**Matt was**
**he'd been**

He'd like to kiss Doria and smear that perfectly applied lipstick. He'd like to bury his fingers in her hair until it was in tangled disarray. He'd like to crush her up against him until her linen suit was as wrinkled as a poplin shirt after a hard day. He'd like to watch those big blue eyes fill with passion and hear her soft voice begging him for more. And then he'd—

*Need to be taken out and shot!* Why in hell was he fantasizing about Doria? He wasn't a horny sixteen-year-old virgin any longer. He was a man with a sensible head on his shoulders and a pair of size-twelve feet firmly grounded in reality.

She might look like a dream. But he knew the reality.

Dear Reader,

Temptation is Harlequin's boldest, most sensuous romance series . . . a series for the 1990s! Fast-paced, humorous, adventurous, these stories are about men and women falling in love—and making the ultimate commitment.

Nineteen ninety-two marks the debut of Rebels & Rogues, our yearlong salute to the Temptation hero. In these twelve exciting books—one a month—by popular authors, including Jayne Ann Krentz, Barbara Delinsky and JoAnn Ross, you'll meet men like Josh—who swore *never* to play the hero. Matt—a hard man to forget . . . an even *harder* man not to love. Cameron—a rogue *not* of this world. And Jake—a rebel *with* a cause.

Twelve rebels and rogues—men who are rough around the edges, but incredibly sexy. Men full of charm, yet ready to fight for the love of a very special woman. . . .

I hope you enjoy Rebels & Rogues, plus all the other terrific Temptation novels coming in 1992!

Warm regards,

Birgit Davis-Todd
Senior Editor

P.S. We love to hear from our readers!

# The Hood

CARIN RAFFERTY

Harlequin Books

TORONTO • NEW YORK • LONDON
AMSTERDAM • PARIS • SYDNEY • HAMBURG
STOCKHOLM • ATHENS • TOKYO • MILAN
MADRID • WARSAW • BUDAPEST • AUCKLAND

Published February 1992

ISBN 0-373-25481-4

THE HOOD



Printed in U.S.A.

# 1

DORIA SINCLAIR. It was a name from Matt Cutter's adolescence, and one he'd thought—no, *hoped*—he'd never hear again. Leaning back in his chair, he frowned at his secretary, Uless Griffith, certain he'd misunderstood him.

"Did you say that Doria Sinclair is in the reception room?"

Uless nodded and snapped his gum—a habit Matt found annoying but managed to ignore. The young man was one of his projects from the ghetto. Last week they'd made a bet on who could stop smoking and the loser had to cough up five hundred bucks. Matt had never been able to stop smoking for longer than a month and knew he'd lose. He hoped, however, that by the time he lit up, at least Uless would have kicked the habit.

"I told the lady that you don't see anyone without an appointment, but she says you're old friends," Uless informed him.

Matt's laugh was mirthless. "I guess we are, at that. What does she want?"

Uless gave an indifferent shrug. "Said it was personal."

"That figures." Matt spun his chair around and gazed out the window. It provided him with a deplorable view of the garbage-strewn alley behind the building. Still, the view was poetically appropriate. The last time he'd seen Doria, she'd been ducking into an alley just like it, leaving him to face the police alone.

The memory caused all the old anger he'd felt toward her to surface, and he unconsciously curled his hands into fists. Intellectually, he didn't hold her responsible for her actions. Emotionally, however, he couldn't forgive her.

Why was she here? What could she possibly want after all this time? If he had any common sense, he'd personally escort her out of the building, but curiosity got the best of him. If it really was Doria, he had to see her; but he needed to get his anger under control first.

He swung back around to face his desk. "Give me ten minutes and then send her in. And, Uless, keep an eye on anything of value, particularly if it's portable. I'm afraid that my good friend has a well-deserved reputation for ripping people off."

Uless eyed his boss with curiosity. When Matt didn't elaborate, he left. The moment the door closed behind him, Matt snuck a handful of shelled sunflower seeds from his top drawer and popped them into his mouth. Uless had substituted gum for his habit. Matt had become a closet sunflower-seed eater.

He wasn't sure why he didn't want Uless to know about his new vice. He supposed it was because it showed a lack of willpower, which translated into a lack of control. He prided himself in always being in control. As long as he was master of his own destiny, the Doria Sinclairs of the world couldn't screw him up.

Unfortunately, he wasn't as convinced by the assertion as he should have been. Suddenly he wanted a cigarette badly.

DORIA STUDIED the black-and-white abstract painting hanging on Matt's reception-room wall. It looked like an inkblot, and not a very good one at that. Funny, but she would have thought Matt would have better taste. Of course, he'd only been sixteen when she'd last seen him, and his taste in art had run more toward pinup girls, particularly of the *Playboy* variety.

As she continued to eye the painting, she decided that maybe it was more reminiscent of a Rorschach test. Ironically, that would be morbidly apropos in this bizarre situation. Who would have believed that two kids from the streets of East Los Angeles would be reunited as a certified public accountant and an Internal Revenue Service treasury agent?

When her boss had handed her the Halliford Company file yesterday and said their audit would be conducted at their accountant's office, she hadn't thought much about it. Companies often preferred that their accountant handle an IRS audit. Then Doria learned that their accountant was Matthew P. Cutter. She'd been convinced that *their* Matthew P. Cutter and *her* Matthew P. Cutter couldn't possibly be the same, but a little discreet sleuthing had revealed that they were.

The moment she confirmed his identity, Doria had panicked. It was possible Matt could still be holding a grudge and would refuse to work with her. She could only imagine her boss's reaction if he learned that when she was fourteen years old, she'd let Matt take the fall for stealing a car that she'd stolen. If Matt was going to be a problem—and gut instinct insisted that he was—she wanted to know so she could decide how to handle him. Matt knew the truth about her past. In a matter of minutes, he could not only destroy the life of respectability she'd spent ten years creating for herself, but he could endanger her job as an IRS agent. Doria was determined that that wasn't going to happen.

She glanced around the room, trying to get a feel for the man Matt had become. Her contacts had assured her that Matt was one of the most sought-after CPA's in the city. Yet, his office was located in a neighborhood that was barely a step above the ghetto where they'd grown up.

Knowing the insanely high rents in Los Angeles, she could have justified the location if the inside of his office was representative of an up-and-coming CPA. Instead it was a mix of new and old. The sofa she sat on was made of plush wine velvet, but the scarred oak coffee table sitting in front of it looked like a reject from the Salvation Army. A top-of-the-line computer sat on the secretary's desk, which was so similar to her own sturdy, gray metal desk at work that she was sure Matt had bought it at a government auction. A half-dozen gray metal filing cabinets, which also looked like government surplus, were behind the desk. They were so battered she was surprised the drawers would close. In contrast, the light gray carpeting was as thick and plush as the sofa, and tempting enough to make her want to kick off her shoes and bury her toes in it.

Baffled by the hodgepodge office decor, Doria returned her gaze to the painting. Just what type of man *had* Matt become?

"Ms. Sinclair?"

Doria jerked her head toward the young black man, who had introduced himself as Matt's secretary, Uless Griffith. He couldn't be more than eighteen or nineteen years old, but his dark eyes held the world-weary cynicism of a man who'd lived long and hard. He was easily six and a half feet tall. His body was rail-thin and his face had a gaunt look. Shaved on the right side of his close-cropped hair was an unfamiliar design that looked like a cross between a lightning bolt and a pitchfork. His clothes were clean but ill-fitting and threadbare, and there was a defiant air about him.

A shiver of uneasiness rushed through Doria. She wouldn't have wanted to meet Uless on the street after dark, but it wasn't the aura of danger surrounding him that made her uptight. From the moment she'd laid eyes on him, he'd struck a chord of recognition inside her. He was a specter from her past—a past she'd been running from for ten years. She had the apprehensive feeling that it was about to catch up with her.

Uless was eyeing her with an expression that was both puzzled and wary. Matt must have told him to throw her out. She'd suspected that he might refuse to see her and was tempted to push her way past Uless and into his office. She decided against it. Such an act would give Matt legitimate cause to refuse to work with her. It would also mean that she'd have to explain to her boss why she'd paid Matt an unofficial visit the day before she was officially scheduled to begin work here.

Frustration flowed through her and she wanted to curse. But respectable women did not swear or cause scenes. She prided herself on being the quintessence of respectability.

"Let me guess. Matt said to throw me out and never let me back in," she stated in her most businesslike tone as she rose to her feet. She slung her purse over her shoulder and headed for the door. "You can tell him to expect me back tomorrow in an official capacity that won't allow him to throw me out."

Uless followed her and held the door shut when she tried to pull it open. Startled, Doria jerked her head up, and she shivered again. Standing this close to him only emphasized his intimidating height.

"Matt's going to see you," he told her. "You're just going to have to hang around for a few minutes."

Doria murmured a surprised "Oh." If Matt was going to see her, then why had Uless been looking at her so strangely?

"Would you like some coffee?" he asked.

"No, thanks." She'd downed so much coffee while bolstering her courage to come here that she'd be wired for a week.

Uless was still hovering over her. Needing to gain some distance, she wandered over to the painting she'd been studying. It didn't look any better close up. Why would Matt hang something so atrocious on his wall?

Peripherally, she noted Uless was beginning to hover again, so she said, "This is a very. . . um, interesting painting. Is it worth anything?"

"It's worth a fortune, and if it disappears, you'll be the primary suspect," a deep voice drawled.

Doria spun around, her eyes widening as her gaze flicked over one of the most handsome men she'd ever seen. He was leaning against the doorjamb behind Uless's desk. His stance emphasized his broad-shouldered, narrow-hipped physique, clad in a tight-fitting black T-shirt and denims so worn they were almost white. His dark brown hair was unconventionally long, and he wore it brushed back at the sides and away from his broad forehead. His nose was straight and narrow. His jaw was square, and his jutting chin had a movie-star cleft in it.

It was his slumberous green eyes, however, that caught Doria's attention. She'd know them anywhere. It really was Matt! She was suddenly flooded with a feeling of warmth so strong, so poignant, she wanted to race across the room and throw herself into his arms. Thankfully, Matt didn't look receptive, which quelled the impulse. Even if he no longer had ill feelings toward her, such a display of affection was taboo. As an IRS agent assigned to audit his client, she couldn't do anything that could be misconstrued as a conflict of interest.

She pointedly ignored Matt's intimation that she'd steal from him, and forced herself to smile widely as she walked toward him. If they were going to trade barbs, she'd rather do it in the privacy of his office. "How are you Matt?"

"I was fine until Uless told me Doria Sinclair was paying me a visit. It makes a man a bit nervous when his infamous past sneaks up on him unexpectedly."

Doria noted the wariness in his eyes. It hurt, but what had she expected? He'd almost landed in a juvenile detention center because of her. "Surprise attacks have always been my trademark."

"More like surprise massacres," Matt rejoined dryly as his eyes flicked over her. If he'd passed her on the street, he probably wouldn't have recognized her and wasn't sure he'd have wanted to. She looked like a walking advertisement for Yuppiedom—a way of life he found nauseating.

But despite her designer-label facade, she'd become a very attractive woman. Her short, red-gold hair framed an oval face with flawless alabaster skin. Her large round eyes were a riveting blue. Her lips were as full and generous as her lush figure, which was revealed by a form-fitting beige linen suit. "It's been a long time, Doria."

"Fourteen years," Doria responded, trembling slightly beneath his bold appraisal. She told herself that it was just the excitement of seeing an old childhood friend, but she knew it was a lie. There had never been anything sexual between them, but she'd been secretly in love with Matt. He'd befriended her when she'd needed a friend the most. He'd tried to protect her from her father when no one else had given a damn. He'd always been there for her, and she'd repaid his kindness by leaving him to face the police alone. The weight of her perfidy had never felt heavier than it did at this moment, particularly when she couldn't find a spark of the old warmth of friendship in Matt's eyes.

When she extended her hand and Matt ignored it with a disparaging smile, Doria knew he hadn't forgiven her. Her common sense told her to leave, but her survival instincts overrode it. Somehow, she had to make peace with him. If she didn't, he could destroy everything.

"Come in to my office," Matt said with exaggerated politeness as he gestured for her to precede him. "Would you like some coffee?"

At that point Doria would have welcomed a cup of coffee. She was so agitated she could have used the cup to occupy her hands. One look at Matt's face, however, assured her that his offer had been made out of habit. She suspected he was regretting it.

"No, thanks. I've had my limit for the day."

Matt automatically watched the natural sway of Doria's hips as she walked ahead of him. He gave a deprecating shake of his head when he experienced a tug of sexual interest. As a teenager, he'd often walked behind Doria just to see that view, and he had to admit that it had improved with age.

As he rounded his desk, he also recalled how he'd used to lie awake at night thinking about stealing a kiss from her. He'd never tried to carry out the fantasy. He'd been too afraid she'd deck him, and he'd been witness to her mean right punch more than once. In fact, the first time he'd met her, she'd been in a fight with two boys who were trying to steal an apple from her. Before Matt could come to her assistance, she'd disabled one by kneeing him in the groin. She'd punched the other in the jaw so hard that Matt had been sure she'd broken her hand. It was evident she hadn't when the boys scurried away, howling expletives at her while she calmly munched on her apple.

He was pulled away from the memory when Doria said, "I hear that you've come up in the world, Matt."

"That's the price one pays for hard work and associating with law-abiding citizens," he stated tersely as he dropped into his chair and lifted his feet to his desk. He eyed her distrustfully when he realized that for a moment, he'd begun to have sentimental feelings about her. That was not only dangerous but stupid. Doria was a manipulator, and he had no idea why she was here. Until he did, he had to be on his guard.

Doria stared in disbelief at the scuffed cowboy boots Matt propped on his desk. Good heavens, all the man needed was a leather jacket and a motorcycle and he'd be James Dean reincarnated! Up-and-coming CPA's weren't supposed to look like this. Actually, *no* CPA was supposed to look like this. They were supposed to be the epitome of the three-piece-suit businessman.

She glanced around his office. It looked worse than his reception area. His huge wooden desk had so much graffiti carved into it that it was difficult to tell what kind of wood it was made from. The chair she was sitting in was comfortable, but its upholstery was badly worn. The only other furnishings in the room were a half-dozen of those weird inkblot paintings hanging on the wall.

Again, Doria was disconcerted. CPA's took care of people's money, which meant they were supposed to inspire trust. Having a graffiti-covered desk that would probably border on pornography if carefully inspected, and a male secretary who looked as if he carried a switchblade, didn't inspire trust. Matt's own dress code certainly didn't improve the image. Good heavens, he might as well have Embezzlers, Incorporated engraved on his door!

"It sounds as if you haven't forgiven me for getting you arrested for joyriding," she responded to his sardonic insinuation that she was not a law-abiding citizen.

"I was arrested for grand theft auto," Matt corrected with a scowl. "The district attorney wanted to try me as an adult.

He and the cops assumed that because I was a boy, I had stolen the car, and they wanted to make an example of me."

Feeling defensive and hating it, Doria shifted uneasily in her chair. "You were barely sixteen. They would never have tried you as an adult. The worst that would have happened was that they'd have tossed you into a juvenile-delinquent center for a few months."

"That's supposed to make me feel better?" Matt drawled sarcastically. "Dammit, Doria, you stole that car!"

"You knew it was stolen, so why did you get into it?" she shot back, and was immediately appalled. He'd yelled at her, and she'd unconsciously yelled back. She *never* raised her voice! It was a sign of ill-breeding. She lowered her voice to a polite level. "I didn't exactly twist your arm to get you into that car."

Matt's scowl deepened, though he couldn't decide if he was irritated because she was right or because she looked and sounded so prim and proper. It made him want to dig at her. To destroy that Yuppie image. To bring out the street fighter that he knew was beneath the surface.

"Yes, I knew it was stolen," he conceded begrudgingly. "But that doesn't change the fact that you took off and left me there to face the police alone. Why did you do that, Doria? And when you found out how much trouble I was in, why didn't you step forward and confess?"

Doria gave a confused shake of her head. She didn't know how to explain her actions to Matt. Now that she was an adult, her reasons sounded weak. She had to make him understand, however, and she leaned back in her chair and crossed her legs, unaware that Matt's eyes followed the motion.

Matt became furious with himself when he noted that she had great legs—nicely rounded calves and thighs that would cushion a man as they wrapped around his hips in lovemaking. The overtly sexual thought made him even angrier. He tore his gaze from her legs and leveled it on her face. He'd learned the hard way that Doria couldn't be trusted. He refused to let himself be sucked in by her again, great legs or not.

When Matt's hostile gaze collided with hers, Doria was filled with a sense of dread. This entire scene was worse than she'd anticipated. She should never have come, but her alternative was even more untenable. They were shorthanded at the office. In order to get her boss to take her off the case, she would have to come up with one heck of an excuse. Since there was no way she could confess the truth, she'd have to lie, and she was already living with too many lies.

She sighed in resignation. "As you said, since you were a boy, the cops assumed you were guilty. They wouldn't have believed me if I had stepped forward, and I didn't tell the truth because I didn't want to wound your ego."

"You didn't want to wound my ego?" Matt mocked scornfully. "Come on, Doria. You can do better than that."

"I'm telling you the truth." Doria leaned toward him to add emphasis to her words. "How would you have felt if it had gotten around that a girl was stealing cars for you? Why, you would have been the laughingstock of the neighborhood. And if you hadn't gotten into so much trouble, your cousin in Denver would never have taken you in. You would have been stuck on the streets with the rest of us. When you put it in that light, I did you a favor."

Matt didn't respond, because though her reasoning was convoluted, she was right again. He would have been the laughingstock of the neighborhood, and the cops wouldn't have believed her if she had stepped forward.

As far as being sent to Denver to live with his cousin, that had been both a blessing and a curse. Dan had kicked his butt into line, but Matt had been separated from his parents. His father had died before he'd been able to get his act together, and that haunted him. He knew all too well that his father had blamed himself for his son's failures.

He wanted to tell Doria that. He wanted her to feel as guilty as he did. He wanted her to suffer, but he held his peace. He didn't know if she was capable of remorse, and he wasn't sure how he'd respond if she wasn't.

"Tell me about yourself," he finally said. "Are you still a car thief, or have you graduated to cat burglar?"

Doria would have laughed if he hadn't delivered the question with such a demeaning, caustic edge. It sparked her temper, but she fought it back under control. She was no longer the bitter, troubled girl Matt had known. She was a respectable woman with a respectable job, and she was not going to let him bait her. "Some people feel that I'm leading a life of even worse crime. I'm a treasury agent for the IRS."

Doria was an IRS agent? He would have been less shocked if she'd announced she was an astronaut. "I didn't think you could work for the government if you had a criminal record."

"I had a juvenile record, which doesn't count."

"But why the Internal Revenue Service?" Matt asked, absolutely confounded. By the very nature of its business, the IRS was a world governed by unbending rules and regulations. As far as he was concerned, it was a stifling environment. He couldn't imagine Doria being a part of it. She'd always been a rule-breaker.

"Why are you a certified public accountant?" she countered.

"Because I'm damn good at it."

Instead of responding, she gave an eloquent shrug, sat back in her chair and folded her hands in her lap. Again, her cool control irked Matt. He was sure she was playing a game with him.

"I thought you had to have a college education to work for the IRS," he said.

Doria's chin went up another notch. "You do."

Matt supposed he shouldn't be surprised that she was college educated. There were several excellent state colleges in California that didn't charge tuition, and there was assistance for students who couldn't afford to pay for their books. That was one of the things he tried to pound into the kids he worked with. They might live in the ghetto, but they didn't have to stay there.

"So tell me what happened to you after you got shipped off to the wilds of Colorado," Doria said, interrupting his thoughts.

Matt leaned farther back in his chair, folding his hands behind his head. Did he want to answer? A part of him insisted he should be spiteful and refuse to divulge anything, but that would be childish. "Denver is not as cosmopolitan as Los Angeles, but it's hardly the wilds."

"It looks as if it agreed with you," Doria noted, unable to stop her eyes from taking a survey of the breadth of his chest that his posture emphasized. She experienced a spine-tingling awareness of him. She forced her gaze to the paintings on the wall. Matt might be an attractive man, but he despised her. Even if he didn't, she couldn't become involved with him. He knew too much about her. He could reveal too much. At that reminder, the tingle in her back changed to fear.

"I suppose it did agree with me." Matt watched Doria's face, trying to figure out what was going through her mind. He'd been well aware of her scrutiny of his body, and though it was absurd, he'd liked it. Instead of reveling in the sensation, however, he became suspicious of it. He couldn't trust her.

"How did you end up back in L.A.?" Doria asked, knowing that her curiosity was dangerous but unable to stifle it. Matt had once been the most important person in her life, and she'd missed him terribly after he was gone. So much so, that she'd cried, which in and of itself had been an aberration. As a physically abused child, she'd learned quickly that tears only aggravated her father and made his beatings more violent. In self-defense, she'd lost the capacity to cry.

The memory made her shudder. She forced it away, wishing she wasn't sitting here with Matt. She didn't want to recall the past! She *refused* to recall the past. It was over with and gone. It couldn't hurt her unless she let it.

Though Matt had no idea what Doria was thinking about, he sensed her emotional upheaval—just as he'd been able to sense it when they were kids. Back then, she'd evoked his protective instincts, and the last thing he wanted to feel toward her was protectiveness. She'd proven that she was more than capable of taking care of herself and didn't give a damn who she hurt in the process.

He repressed the urge to ask what was wrong and answered her question. "After I graduated from college, I decided I hated snow, so I came home."

*Home.* The word vibrated through Doria. It was a concept she'd never understood. It conveyed a sense of belonging. As she studied Matt's face, she realized that one of the reasons she'd been drawn to him so many years ago was because he did seem to belong. Not literally, because no one belonged in the ghetto. It was more that he possessed a sense of rightness about himself. As if he knew exactly who he was and was comfortable with it. She'd envied that trait in him then, and she envied it now. He oozed self-confidence, and suddenly she understood why he was so successful, despite his unconventionality.

She also became even more aware of him as a man. She couldn't stop her gaze from traveling from the toes of his scuffed cowboy boots to his chest, noting every masculine line in between. She blushed when she raised her eyes to his face and discovered his fixed on her—unabashed, arrogant and slightly amused.

She glanced quickly away and said, "Who would have believed that two punks from the streets could become so successful?"

"You were the punk," Matt muttered. "I only tagged along."

Doria tilted her head to the side and regarded him thoughtfully. "You know it's true. You never did have the stomach for thievery, so why did you do it?"

"The truth?" Matt rested his elbows on the arms of his chair and steepled his fingers beneath his chin. He knew he was wandering into risky territory, but he wanted to tell her the truth, particularly after she'd just given him the once-over. Again, he'd found he'd liked it, and he was convinced she was interested, which made him want to punish her. Intuitively, he knew this was the way to do it.

"Of course, I want the truth," she answered, leaning toward him expectantly.

"I had a bad crush on you," he said with such mocking insolence that Doria recoiled. He sounded as if he couldn't believe he'd been so stupid, and that hurt so badly that she felt the uncustomary sting of tears. She stared at her hands as she struggled with her unruly emotions. Matt had cared for her more deeply than she'd realized. It made her feel guiltier for what she'd done to him.

If she'd known how he felt about her, would she have handled the car theft differently? She wanted to believe she would have, but there was a part of her that was doubtful. Though the earlier reasons she'd given Matt for her behavior were true, there had been an even more urgent reason for her to abandon him. She'd been in so much trouble up to that point that the juvenile authorities had threatened to put her into a foster home if she was arrested again. That should have made her rush right out and get into trouble, but it had terrified her instead. At least with her father, she'd known what she was faced with. Foster care had been an unknown.

"Why are you here, Doria?" Matt asked curtly. It was time to end their meeting. He could sense her turmoil again and refused to respond to it. She was nothing to him any longer. Whatever was tormenting her was none of his business. The sooner he got her out of his office, the sooner he could forget she even existed.

Doria squirmed in her chair at his question. How he responded to her answer could affect the remainder of her life. "I'm going to be the field agent on the Halliford Company audit. I'll start working here tomorrow."

Matt felt as if he'd just been punched in the stomach. He dropped his feet to the floor and reached for the file lying on the left-hand corner of his desk. He flipped it open, confirming what he already knew. "The letter I received from your office says that Thomas Sanger is the field agent assigned to Halliford's audit."

"Tom had an unexpected family emergency and is on extended leave. Since I'm available, the boss assigned me the case rather than delay it."

*Damn!* Halliford was the grayest client Matt had. It wasn't that they didn't pay their share of taxes or were doing anything illegal, but the nature of their business put them on a shaky line. A few discreet calls had confirmed that Sanger was new in the field. Matt hadn't done much preparing for the audit, because a new agent was more prone to be accepting and not to dig. Experienced field agents were another matter. They'd have tax case after tax case to cite. He'd have to be able to recite just as many conflicting cases in order to convince them that his reasoning was sound. Just how experienced was Doria?

"How long have you been in the field?" he asked, hoping she'd say she was as new as Sanger, but having a sinking feeling that he was in trouble. What else should he have expected? He *was* dealing with Doria.

"Two years," she answered with a quizzical look. "Why?"

"No reason." He cursed inwardly. She was a double whammy. She was experienced in the field, and they were old friends. No, make that *used* to be old friends. That meant that she'd make sure all the *i*'s were dotted and the *t*'s were crossed so no one could accuse her of conflict of interest.

"Do you have a problem working with me?" she asked worriedly. "If you do, I'll step out. All I ask is that you don't tell my boss why. My juvenile record doesn't affect my qualifications, but . . ."

"But it could affect your career," he finished as he regarded her through narrowed eyes.

She gave a fatalistic shrug. "It probably wouldn't, but I'd rather not take the chance. I've worked too hard to get to this point, and I'd hate to have it messed up over crimes I committed before the age of fifteen."

*Not to mention that the entire office would discover that I'm a master liar,* she thought. As far as her friends and coworkers were concerned, she'd been raised in a normal middle-class home with all the middle-class trappings. She even took a vacation once a year for the obligatory "trip to Florida to visit her retired parents." Then she spent the entire week hiding out in her apartment for fear someone she knew would see her.

She'd begun creating her fictional life when she'd started college, because she'd seen how the other students reacted to kids from the ghetto. They eyed them with a mixture of pity and distrust. If they did befriend them, it was as if they were doing so to defy convention and do something dangerous. By the time she'd graduated, she'd become so comfortable with the lie that she'd almost forgotten it was one. Over the years it had perpetuated itself. Now, she couldn't get out of it if she wanted to, and she didn't want to. She liked the sense of respectability it gave her. It was her way of belonging.

Matt eyed Doria, assessing her. This was the perfect opportunity for him to get his revenge against her. But even as that thought ran through Matt's mind, he dismissed it. It would violate the code of the streets, and though he had revised the code as he'd matured, he still upheld it. In its own way, it did have a moral foundation. Besides, it was evident that Doria was uncomfortable around him. Having to work with him on a daily basis might be enough to satisfy his need to punish her. It would also be interesting to see how she reacted to Halliford's unusual merchandise—which should rattle her polished, Yuppie exterior.

"I don't have a problem with you doing the audit," he told her. "I'm just surprised that you've accepted the case. Halliford is a rather . . . unique business."

"What's so unique about them?" Doria inquired suspiciously. Matt sounded almost friendly. Considering his earlier hostility, she suspected that he was up to something. Since she'd only been assigned the case yesterday afternoon, she hadn't had time for more than a cursory review of Halliford's file. They appeared to be an average mail-order company. So, why was Matt looking so smug?

She became even more suspicious when he propped his feet back on his desk and drawled laconically, "If you don't know, I'm not going to tell you. I guess you'll find out to-morrow."

# 2

"ULESS, I WANT EVERY Halliford file we've got in my office in five minutes," Matt ordered, the moment Doria was gone. "And you're working late tonight. Got a problem with that?"

"Not if I'm being paid overtime," Uless answered.

Matt gave him a grim smile. "Consider yourself on triple time. By tomorrow morning we have to have every detail of Halliford's business committed to memory."

Uless popped another piece of gum into his mouth. "Why? What's happening tomorrow?"

"Ms. Doria Sinclair, treasury field agent for the IRS, is going to be our guest."

He strode back into his office, snatched up his phone and hit the Memory key for Halliford. When their controller came on the line, he rattled off a list of records he'd need and emphasized that the matter was urgent. The man assured him that they'd be delivered within the hour.

Uless dropped a stack of files on Matt's desk when he hung up the phone. "Here's everything on Halliford. I thought Sanger was going to do the audit."

"Sanger has a family emergency." Matt sat down and cursed when he reached into the pocket of his T-shirt for a cigarette and came up empty. He glowered at Uless's sly grin. He'd get through this cramming session without smoking if it killed him. He wasn't going to part with five hundred dollars that easily. "Doria's his replacement, and she has two years' experience in the field."

Uless folded his long frame into the chair in front of Matt's desk. "So, what's the big deal? You told me that you never do anything illegal."

"I don't, but the tax laws are open to interpretation. The more experience an agent has in the field, the more likely he—or she, in this case—will challenge my interpretations."

"I still don't see why it's such a big deal. If you and the lady are friends . . ."

"Don't even finish that thought," Matt admonished sternly. "Doria would never let friendship interfere with her work, and I'd never use a friend like that."

"Hey, don't go all high-and-mighty on me," Uless said, holding his hands up in mock surrender. "It was just a thought."

"Well, it wasn't a very good one," Matt grumbled, though he wasn't sure if he was grumbling at Uless or himself. The word *friend* had come too easily when he'd been referring to Doria. In actuality, he should have choked on it. He had a feeling that this little game of revenge he'd started had the potential of backfiring on him. That meant he needed to keep his guard up more than ever. He also needed to concentrate on Halliford's records if he was going to be prepared for Doria. That would be a hell of a lot easier if he had a carton of cigarettes.

"I'll put on a fresh pot of coffee," Uless said as he stood.

"Put on two pots," Matt advised while grabbing his books on tax regulations, tax cases and the first file on the stack Uless had given him. Then he snuck a handful of sunflower seeds from his drawer and chewed them murderously.

ON THE DRIVE BACK to her office, Doria wondered what she was going to find out about Halliford tomorrow. By the time she reached her office, she had a sneaky suspicion that she was being set up by her boss.

She grabbed the Halliford file and flipped it open the moment she reached her desk. She didn't have to dig far before she discovered the meaning of Matt's words. With a heartfelt groan she plopped into her chair.

"Somebody dying over there?" Kathy Adams asked as she peered over the top of the partition separating them. Kathy had been a treasury agent for more than twenty years. When Doria had first come on the job, she'd feared that Kathy might consider her a rival. She'd soon learned that Kathy didn't have an adversarial bone in her body. She'd taken Doria under her wing and they'd become great friends.

"Get down off that rickety Peeping Tom's stool before you fall and break your arthritic neck," Doria said with a fond grin. "And then come on over. You won't believe what Dryer's done to me this time."

Kathy disappeared and walked into Doria's cubicle seconds later. She shoved a stack of papers aside and perched on the edge of Doria's desk. Their boss didn't allow anything as frivolous as an extra chair in a cubicle. He felt it encouraged fraternization.

"So, what's up?" Kathy asked.

Doria handed her the file. "Check out page five."

Kathy flipped quickly to the page in question and burst into roaring laughter.

"Since you think it's so funny, why don't we exchange cases?" Doria suggested slyly.

"No, thanks." Kathy handed Doria the file. "It might give my husband some naughty ideas, and he's naughty enough as it is."

Doria chuckled. Kathy and her husband had been married thirty-eight years, which Doria found amazing. Kathy, who stood at five foot nothing and weighed barely a hundred pounds, didn't look a day over forty. The truth was, she was fast approaching sixty and was a grandmother to a half-dozen adorable tots. She claimed that she looked so young because of a regular visit to her hairdresser, who gave her short chestnut locks eternal youth. Doria preferred to believe that it was Kathy's reward for being a truly nice person.

Kathy sobered suddenly. "Hey, is this case offensive to you? If it is, you march right into Dryer's office and tell him to give it to someone else."

"I wouldn't give him the satisfaction," Doria declared as she considered her relationship with her boss. Dryer called her The Kid, and a few times he'd had the audacity to pat her on the head. With anyone else, she would have been furious, but she knew Dryer couldn't help himself. He was from the era when women were expected to stay at home, not pursue careers. He was also constantly telling her that she reminded him of his "little girl," who was ten years older than Doria. She found it ironic that she could remind him of his daughter, yet he'd hand her a case like Halliford Company's.

"And it's not that I find the case offensive," she assured Kathy. "So, their primary business is selling costumes to exotic dancers? Those people have to get their pasties and jockstraps from somewhere. It's just that..."

"Just that what?" Kathy prodded when Doria didn't continue.

Kathy was the closest Doria had ever come to having a confidante, but how could she explain her predicament with Matt without revealing her past? She couldn't, and she knew that Kathy would be disappointed if she found out Doria had lied to her.

"Well?" Kathy said in exasperation when Doria still didn't speak.

"Halliford's CPA is an old childhood friend," Doria admitted, and then quickly added, "And we were strictly friends. I was only fourteen when I knew him."

Kathy nodded in understanding. "I can see where that would be a problem. When you look at him, you feel fourteen again. The thought of discussing pasties and jockstraps with him embarrasses you."

*I wish it was that simple,* Doria thought. Unfortunately, she didn't feel fourteen when she looked at Matt. She felt exactly like a twenty-eight-year-old woman should feel around an attractive man. But Matt despised her, and even if he didn't, he was the last man she could ever become involved with. He could destroy her credibility in a matter of minutes.

"You've got me figured out," she said.

"Well, don't worry, kid," Kathy replied as she jumped off Doria's desk and gave her shoulder a reassuring squeeze. "You'll do just fine."

She walked out of the cubicle, and then quickly stuck her head back in. "By the way, I've always wanted to know how a stripper keeps those pasties on, and if it hurts when she pulls them off. If it doesn't, I may try it out on Herb. So, see what you can find out."

Doria laughed and threw her tissue box at Kathy's disappearing head.

MATT WAS EXHAUSTED after a marathon night with Halliford's records. As he climbed onto his motorcycle and drove to the office, he considered himself as prepared as he could be—that is, for anything Doria might throw at him. Of course, she probably wouldn't throw much at him for a couple of days. He generally stuck an IRS agent in the back office with all the files and told them where the coffeepot was. Then he left them alone for a day or two. By that time they were either totally confused or so bored they welcomed his company.

But Doria wasn't the normal IRS agent, and he would have to make a concerted effort to treat her as such. That might be easier said than done, since he'd spent half of last night reliving the past.

He wanted to hate Doria, because it would justify his anger toward her. The more he'd remembered, however, the harder it was to stay angry. She'd been troubled and reckless, but who wouldn't be when your only living relative was a father who'd just as soon punch you in the mouth as draw a breath?

Matt, whose own parents had been gentle and loving, had never understood why Doria's father abused her. If the man had had an addiction to alcohol or drugs, he would have at least felt as if there were a reason. He could even have accepted it if he'd felt that Sinclair was just plain mean. But Doria was the only one who provoked his violence. Matt had always suspected that she knew why, but she'd never talked about it.

Matt kept telling himself that it didn't matter why Doria had been abused. He kept reminding himself how she had betrayed him. He kept recalling the look of defeat on his father's face the day he'd left for Denver. He'd been so angry at being sent away that he'd refused to tell his father goodbye and that he loved him. And then it was too late to do either.

As the regrets began to overwhelm him, Matt's anger toward Doria revived. He welcomed it. It was easier to deal with than remorse. It also reassured him that he'd be able to keep his distance from her. He'd spent too many hours last night thinking about what an attractive woman she'd become, and the sexual pull he felt toward her was dangerous. When the libido kicked into gear, the brain got soft. The next thing you knew, you were out of control.

He pulled into his reserved parking space, dug a handful of sunflower seeds from the bag in his jacket pocket and tossed them into his mouth. He'd already downed half the bag and still had a full workday ahead of him. At this rate, he'd soon be up to three or four bags a day. Hell, it was cheaper to smoke.

"Morning, Uless," he said when he walked into his office.

"Coffee's already on," Uless told him without glancing up from the magazine he was reading. "I took pity on you and brought in some blueberry muffins."

Matt headed for the coffee closet. "You're a man after my own heart."

"Don't take this wrong," Uless called after him, "but you aren't my type. Your curves aren't in the right places."

"Does this mean the engagement's off?" Matt joked as he wandered back into the room.

"Afraid so."

"What are you reading?" Matt asked as he sat down on the sofa Doria had occupied the day before and bit into his muffin. His gaze wandered to the painting she had called "interesting." He'd been able to tell by her tone that she hadn't liked it. He couldn't figure out why. As far as he was concerned, abstract art was unbeatable. It allowed you to use your imagination. It could be anything you wanted it to be. Besides, the artist who'd done this painting and the half-dozen others in his office was hot, which made the paintings a good investment.

"The emotional needs of women in love," Uless mumbled.

"What?" Matt queried in confusion.

"I'm reading about the emotional needs of women in love," Uless repeated. "This psychologist says that if a man wants to understand a woman's romantic needs, he should read some romance novels. You ever read a romance novel?"

Matt snickered as he propped his feet on the coffee table. "Not the kind that psychologist is talking about. I'm not into euphemisms."

Uless leaned back in his chair and mimicked Matt by putting his feet up on his desk. "Well, you have to admit that it's an interesting premise. Take Sally," he said, referring to his girlfriend. "Her nose is always stuck in one of those romances. She must be getting something out of them."

"Yeah. Escapism," Matt responded. "But escapism isn't reality, and if you try to act like a romantic hero, you're going to fall flat on your butt. Just do what comes naturally, Uless, and your love life will be fine. Take my word for it."

This time, Uless snickered. "It's hard to take the word of a man who hasn't had a date in six months. I'm getting worried about you, Matt. A man can't live on work alone. He needs a little lovin' to soften the edges."

"My edges are just fine." Matt yawned, then glanced down at his watch. "Doria should be here any minute. Did you put the Halliford files in the back office?"

"Yep," Uless replied, then added, "Matt, I know it's probably none of my business, but yesterday you said this lady treasury agent has a reputation for ripping people off. Is that true?"

"Yeah, but that was a long time ago. Doria's one of us."

Uless gaped at him. "That piece of fluff came off the streets?"

"Fourteen years ago, that piece of fluff could have knocked your teeth down your throat," Matt replied dryly. "She could have also stolen the gum right out of your mouth without you knowing it."

"Well, I'll be damned!" Uless murmured in awe.

At that very moment, Doria walked in. Matt's gaze automatically surveyed her. She looked thoroughly professional in a lime-green suit with matching pumps. She also looked like a million other businesswomen in Los Angeles. He'd seen Barbie dolls with more individuality.

"Good morning, Doria," he drawled, not bothering to rise to his feet. "We have Halliford's records ready for your inspection. Would you like a cup of coffee and a blueberry muffin before we get you settled in?"

Doria was so shocked by the sight of Matt that she couldn't answer. He was dressed the same as yesterday, except the denims he wore today had one knee ripped out. He'd added a pair of mirrored sunglasses, which were pushed to the top of his head, and a black leather jacket to his ensemble. He really was James Dean reincarnated, and something hot and reckless stirred inside her.

Startled by the feeling, she took a quick step back and stared at him in bewilderment. What was wrong with her? She didn't respond to men like Matt, and she certainly wasn't reckless! Everything she did, everything she said, was steeped in conventionality. To fit into acceptable society, your life had to be ordinary and commonplace. There was nothing ordinary and commonplace about Matt, and there never would be.

She didn't realize she'd been staring until Matt murmured mockingly, "Like what you see?" He gave her a brazen appraisal, and then grinned insolently. "You'd do in a pinch, but I prefer my women a bit more mussed."

He was purposely heckling her. Her first impulse was to say something rude and scathing, but her common sense surfaced. She was here to do a job—not spar with Matt.

She set her briefcase and laptop computer on the sofa next to him. "Lucky for you, I'm not a pinch hitter. Where do I find the coffee and muffins?"

"If you remember your manners and say good-morning to Uless, I'll take you to them," he replied.

Doria had been so absorbed with Matt that she hadn't noticed the young man. She winced at the realization that Uless had heard her and Matt's barbed exchange.

"Good morning, Uless. I'm sorry I didn't greet you earlier, but I didn't see you sitting there."

"That's okay." He snapped his gum and gave a dismissive wave of his hand. "I'm easy to miss. I just fade right into the woodwork. Makes it harder for Matt to get a decent day's work out of me."

"You wish," Matt muttered as he dropped his feet to the floor and stood. "Coffee's this way, Doria. Feel free to help yourself while you're here. The only rule we have is that the person who empties the pot makes the next one."

"That's a joke," Uless scoffed. "Matt always leaves enough to cover the bottom so he doesn't have to make the next pot."

"Hey, sometimes you gotta bend the rules so they work in your favor," Matt defended. He headed for the coffee closet without checking to see if Doria was following. Of course, he didn't need to check, because the scent of her perfume remained constant. It was an unfamiliar fragrance—a delicate bouquet that was both pleasing and tantalizing to the senses.

"Here we are," he said, stopping so abruptly that Doria nearly ran into him. He turned to face her. "I don't suppose you brought your own mug."

"No, but I'll be sure to do so tomorrow," Doria replied. Matt was standing so close to her that she had to tilt her head back to see his face. She'd realized he was tall, but she hadn't realized how tall. At five foot seven, she found it unusual to be looking this far up at a man.

"Whatever," Matt murmured as he stared down at her. Yesterday, he'd noticed that her skin was flawless, but he hadn't noticed how translucent it was. He told himself that it was a trick of the light or, more likely, the modern miracle of makeup. That didn't make it any less sensual. He wanted to brush the back of his hand against her cheek, trail his thumb over her bottom lip.

Who was he trying to kid? He'd like to kiss her and smear that perfectly applied lipstick. He'd like to bury his fingers in her hair until it was in tangled disarray. He'd like to crush her up against him until she was as wrinkled as a poplin shirt after a hard day. He'd like to watch those big blue eyes fill with passion, and hear her soft voice begging him for more. And then he'd—

*Need to be taken out and shot!* Why in hell was he fantasizing about Doria? He wasn't a sixteen-year-old horny virgin any longer. He was a man with a sensible head on his shoulders and a pair of size-twelve feet firmly grounded in reality. She might look like a dream, but he knew differently.

"Are you sure you aren't a pinch hitter?" he taunted, immediately regretting the words when first hurt and then anger flared into her eyes.

She marched into the coffee closet, and Matt cursed himself for goading her. Regardless of his feelings for her, he had to think of his client. He didn't think she'd be petty enough to take it out on Halliford if she was upset with him, but he'd never have believed that she'd desert him fourteen years ago, either.

"Doria, I'm sorry. That was uncalled-for." He stepped into the room and grabbed her arm to gain her attention.

She jerked away from his touch so violently that she slammed her hip into the wall. Then she spun around to face him, her face pale and her eyes wild.

"Don't ever grab me like that again," she whispered harshly.

"I won't. I'm sorry. I forgot," Matt soothed. He had honestly forgotten her frenzied reaction to being grabbed—a reflex brought on by her father's constant abuse. He'd also forgotten how unnerving it was to see her respond to his touch like that. "You hit the wall pretty hard. Are you okay?"

Doria nodded, because she was shaking so badly inside that she couldn't trust her voice. It had been years since she'd reacted like that to someone's touch. Then again, it had been years since anyone had grabbed her. Thankfully it had happened with Matt, so she wouldn't have to give an explanation.

"Here, drink this." Matt pressed a half-filled mug of coffee laced heavily with milk into her hands, his expression concerned.

Doria wanted to tell him to go away. His solicitousness grated, because she knew it was brought on by pity. She despised being pitied. She also knew his concern would disappear the moment he knew she was all right.

But she was still so rattled that she accepted the coffee. Matt had poured so much milk into it that it was only lukewarm. She drained the mug while trying to figure out how to get out of this mess with her dignity intact.

Matt watched Doria drink her coffee with a mixture of emotions, a good portion of which was fury at Doria's father, mixed with a hefty dollop of disgust with himself. As a kid he'd known Doria's plight. He'd done what he could to protect her, but now he realized that he should have told his parents what was going on. He hadn't because Doria had begged him not to. At sixteen, he'd been more eager to please her than to do what was right.

"How did you cope with your father after I left?" he asked gruffly.

"Leave it alone, Matt," she pleaded. She didn't want to take a journey into the past. She *couldn't* take a journey into the past. It hurt too badly.

"I don't want to leave it alone. Were you okay? Did your father hurt you?"

"No more than he ever did," she answered bitterly. "And it got better. After you left, I started hanging out at the library. He couldn't afford to cause much of a disturbance there."

"And where is he now?"

"Where he's always been. Living in hell," she stated matter-of-factly. "How about one of those blueberry muffins?"

"What does 'Living in hell' mean? Is he dead?"

"Yes!" Doria lied, not about to tell Matt the truth. He'd only ask more questions, and her father was one subject she couldn't discuss with anyone. "He's stone-cold dead. Now, may I have a blueberry muffin?"

Their gazes met—his challenging, hers defiant. Matt glanced away first and handed her a muffin. She wandered out to Uless's office, acknowledging she should try to get off this case. She'd been here less than fifteen minutes and already felt wrung out. As the days passed, it would only get worse. Matt wasn't going to leave the past alone, and she couldn't bear to relive it. There was too much pain and too much anger. She feared that if she ever faced those feelings head-on, they'd be so overwhelming that they'd destroy her.

She only had to look at Uless to know he'd heard what had happened between her and Matt. That infuriated her. If Matt wanted to confront her, he should at least have the courtesy to do so in privacy. He didn't have to broadcast her life to the entire world!

"Why don't you have a seat, Doria?" Matt suggested.

Doria started at the sound of his voice and nearly spilled her coffee. She hadn't seen him enter the room. She glanced over her shoulder. He was watching her cautiously, as if he expected her to do something dramatic, like faint at his feet. That made her angrier. She wasn't some hothouse flower that had to be coddled!

She wanted to rail at him and might have done so if the telephone hadn't rung, reinserting sanity. She was here on a professional basis, and she was going to behave like a professional if it killed her.

"I think I should get to work," she stated coolly. "Unlike you, I don't charge exorbitant prices for my time. I'm on salary and earn every penny of it."

It wasn't Doria's words as much as the haughtiness with which she'd delivered them that lit Matt's temper. Not only had she intimated that he wasn't worth the money he charged, she'd made it sound as if he were cheating his clients! How could he have felt so sorry for her a few minutes ago? There was nothing sorry about her.

He walked to the sofa and retrieved her briefcase and computer, saying stiffly, "Follow me."

He led her down a short hallway to an empty office. Doria was stunned when she stepped into the room. Considering the crazy decor she'd seen so far, she'd expected to be consigned to junk-shop heaven. The room was heaven, all right, but there wasn't a piece of junk in sight. There was a gleaming oak desk with a personal computer off to the side. The walls were a sedate off-white and, to her relief, there were two attractive ocean scenes on the walls instead of inkblots.

As Matt placed her laptop and briefcase on the desk, he said, "Uless will help you in any way he can, Doria, but he goes to school on Monday, Wednesday and Friday afternoons. We're on our own, then. I know you have your own computer, but this computer is at your disposal. If you're unfamiliar with the word-processing program or need anything, talk to Uless. He knows more about what goes on in the office than I do."

Doria barely heard a word he was saying. He moved with such grace, and she couldn't have ignored the enticing ripple of muscle beneath his clothing if she'd wanted to. To her chagrin, what she wanted to do was touch him, and she laced her hands behind her back to keep them out of trouble.

"I'm sure I'll be fine. This is a very nice office."

Matt leaned against the desk, his eyes drifting over her delicate features, conjuring up an image of her at fourteen. Even then, he'd been able to see beneath the grime and the gauntness to the promise of beauty. He'd been attracted to her, but it hadn't been the outer package that appealed to him most. It had been her will to survive, her guts. She hadn't been afraid of anything, not even her father. Well, maybe that wasn't exactly true, but there had always been an air about her that said, "I will endure."

Matt had to admire her. From basically nothing, she'd made herself into something, and he intuitively knew that she'd done it on her own. He also sensed that in the transition Doria had lost an important part of herself. He wasn't sure what it was, but it disturbed him.

And *she* was disturbing, he acknowledged as his gaze roamed over her and the sexual tug inside him became more intense. He wanted to believe it was because he hadn't been involved with a woman in ages; but he never lied to himself. His attraction was far more complicated and ultimately more threatening. It involved his past feelings for her, which had been stronger than he wanted to profess.

It dawned on him that he should have refused to work with her, but it was too late to do anything about that now. He'd have to make the best of it. He'd also have to make sure that he maintained his distance. The best way to do that was to provoke her.

"Is there a man in your life?" he asked.

Doria regarded Matt cautiously. Once again, he sounded almost friendly, and yet the last thing he clearly felt toward her was friendship. She considered lying to him, but couldn't bring herself to do so. "No."

"Why not?"

"Not too many men want to become involved with an IRS agent. I think they're afraid that if it doesn't work out, I'll have them audited."

"Would you?" He folded his arms over his chest, drawing Doria's gaze to his bulging biceps. Absently she wondered when he'd removed his jacket. It must have been after she'd left him in the coffee closet.

"Contrary to popular opinion, a treasury agent doesn't have that much power, but if I could, I suppose it would depend upon how angry I was."

Matt was sure he was arguing semantics, but he found it interesting that she'd said "angry" rather than "hurt." Not that a person who'd been hurt didn't become angry. It was Doria's inflection, however, that made him feel as if she'd meant anger on a literal rather than an emotional level. Had she never allowed anyone close enough to hurt her, including himself? Was that why she'd been able to turn her back on him so easily?

"What about you?" she inquired. "Is there a woman in your life?"

"No."

"Why not?"

"Because I demand complete loyalty from a woman, and I have yet to find one capable of giving it," he answered impassively.

As he'd intended, his words hit their mark. Doria again felt the uncustomary sting of tears in her eyes. She shouldn't let him see them, but she couldn't seem to drag her gaze away from his accusing one.

"Why didn't you tell the cops I stole the car?" she asked.

"Because you were my friend. Because I trusted you to do the right thing. Because . . ."

"Because?" Doria prompted when he didn't finish.

Instead of answering, Matt closed his eyes and shook his head. Doria told herself to stay away from him, but beneath his anger she could sense his pain. She couldn't bear the thought that she was the source of it.

"I'm sorry, Matt." She approached him and tentatively touched his arm, expecting him to flinch from her touch, maybe even strike out at her.

What he did was even worse. He opened his eyes and stared at her. At first his gaze was accusatory. Then it began to shift, reflecting reluctance, confusion, and finally desire.

When he wrapped his hand around her arm and pulled her against him, the very gentleness of his hold was punishing. The electrifying touch of his body was reproving, and the knowledge that he was going to kiss her was torture.

They stared at each other, their eyes locked in defiance. Then Matt threaded the fingers of his free hand into her hair and lowered his head. Doria knew he wasn't going to kiss her because he cared for her. It was because he hated her. He couldn't have chosen a crueler penance if he'd tried, because she wanted him to kiss her. It was wrong. It was insane. But it was true.

Matt refused to think about what he was doing as Doria's lips came closer. He concentrated on the delicious curve of her lower lip. The full bow of her upper lip. The teasing enticement of her tongue as it flicked out nervously and then disappeared. When her lips parted in anticipation, he released a sigh that was more a groan. He'd spent so many sexually frustrated hours as a teenager fantasizing about what she'd taste like. Finally, he would know.

"Matt?" Uless said from the doorway.

Doria jumped away from Matt so quickly that she would have fallen if he hadn't still had a grip on her arm. He glanced toward Uless, and then back to Doria, cursing silently at her expression of horror.

Talk about bad timing, or maybe it was good timing! If Uless had arrived a few seconds later, he might have found them in a clinch. He'd never be able to explain kissing a treasury agent who was auditing a client. Why had he been thinking about kissing her in the first place?

"What is it, Uless?" he asked, relieved to realize that though he was inwardly quaking, he sounded perfectly normal.

"Mr. Bauer is here."

"Great. Take him into my office and give him some coffee and a muffin. I'll be there in a minute."

When Uless left, Matt turned back to Doria. She still looked horrified, and that irked him. As his gaze drifted to her lips, however, he couldn't summon up the energy to beleaguer her. "Sorry about that. I'll tell him that it was just a hug between two old friends."

"And you think he'll buy it?" Doria asked skeptically, barely able to refrain from wringing her hands. *Damn!* Why had she let Matt put her in such a position? Why had she put herself in such a position? The rules of professional behavior for a treasury agent were strict and unbending. She could get a reprimand even if she let Matt do something as innocuous as buy her lunch while she was auditing his client. If her boss ever found out that she and Matt had been almost kissing, she'd probably lose her job!

Matt frowned impatiently as Doria's expression became panicked. "Doria, stop looking as if the end of the world is coming. I said I'd tell Uless that it was just a hug between two old friends."

"But will he believe it?" she asked shrilly.

"Probably not, but who cares?"

"I care. Dammit, Matt, we're talking about my livelihood! If he told—"

"Uless wouldn't know who to tell," Matt interrupted crossly. "And even if he did, he wouldn't. Unlike some people I know, he'd never do anything that would cause me trouble."

Before Doria could sputter a retort, Matt stormed out of the office, and her temper erupted. For want of something better to do she kicked the desk leg, cursing when it left a scuff mark across the toe of her new shoe.

She considered going after Matt and having it out with him. What she'd done to him fourteen years ago had been dreadful. Inexcusable. Indefensible. Unpardonable. He had every right to hate her, but she was here to do a job. He was going to treat her like a professional, or she'd... What? Complain to her boss? Fat chance, and Matt knew it. He had her right where he wanted her and there was nothing she could do about it.

With a groan, she collapsed into the desk chair and rubbed at her temples. If she managed to maintain her sanity through this audit, she'd be lucky. And the quicker she got to work, the faster she could get out of here. It was time to stop feeling sorry for herself. She reached for her laptop.

Within moments, she was ready, and she pulled one of Halliford's files from the bottom of the stack. It had been her experience that all the "clean" files were on top and the questionable ones on the bottom. She stuck her pencil behind her ear, noting that the label on the outside said it was Halliford's advertising expenses. That was as good a place to start as any.

She flipped open the file and her jaw dropped at the full-page advertisement for one of Halliford's novelties. The model was a muscle-bound Adonis clad only in a jockstrap, which resembled an elephant, complete with trunk.

Doria slammed the file closed and placed her palms against her burning cheeks. She wasn't a prude, but this was bordering on the absurd! What man in his right mind would wear something so . . . so ridiculous?

She giggled when she reopened the file and read the ad, learning that they also offered a giraffe. Impishly, she wrote down the address and the particulars for ordering the animal duo. They'd make a great gag gift for Kathy.

With that done, she began to work in earnest, though she did burst into frequent laughter over some of Halliford's other unique novelty items. When she came across a list of clients who'd received complimentary elephant and giraffe jockstraps, she perused it, searching for any exceptional large numbers. It didn't happen often, but occasionally she ran across a "gift" that smacked of graft.

The numbers seemed reasonable. She started to lay the list aside, but out of curiosity glanced at the names. Her eyes widened when Matt's leaped out at her. Instinct told her that Matt wouldn't be happy to have knowledge of his unusual underwear bandied about. She just may have come across some ammunition to use in the war he was waging against her.

She'd try to make a truce with him first, but if he refused, she'd threaten to reveal what she'd discovered. CPA's were generally a closemouthed bunch when it came to their clients, but they were not adverse to gossiping about one another. All she'd have to do was mention it to one who was prone to gossip, and every CPA in Southern California would soon be privy to the information. After that, Matt would have a heck of a time maintaining his bad-boy image. Why, it could get so bad that he might be forced into wearing a suit!

Feeling more in control of what had so far been an out-of-control situation, Doria went back to work. She did take a moment, however, to wonder if Matt would do as much justice to his elephant's trunk as the model had. She grinned at the thought, but shook her head to dismiss it. Even if she and Matt were the last two people on earth, his antipathy toward her guaranteed that she'd never have the opportunity to find out.

# 3

WHEN ULESS KNOCKED once and entered the office, Matt had just reached for some sunflower seeds. He nearly slammed his hand in the drawer as he hurriedly closed it. Uless eyed him suspiciously, and Matt nodded in the direction of Doria's office. It was the only way he could think of to keep the young man from accusing him of smoking and demanding to see what he was hiding. "So, how's it going?"

Uless gave him a strained look. "Well, she hasn't asked for anything, but . . ."

"But?" Matt prompted. Uless's tone sounded ominous.

"She's been laughing, Matt, and I mean laughing her head off."

"She's laughing?" Matt repeated incredulously. "What about?"

"I don't have any idea, but I'm telling you, man, it's weird."

"Laughing?" Matt mumbled in mystification as he collapsed back in his chair. He'd expected any number of reactions from Doria once she found out what Halliford sold, but laughter hadn't been one of them.

He supposed it had been a low blow not to warn her ahead of time, and outside of the initial shock, he hadn't expected her to be upset. In the neighborhood they'd grown up in, they'd seen far more bizarre things than any novelty Halliford imported.

"Maybe I should ask her to go to lunch with me," he mused. It would not only give him a chance to appease his curiosity about her laughter, but a chance to apologize for storming out on her this morning. She'd had every right to be concerned about her job. If he hadn't been so confused and frustrated over that damn kiss they'd almost shared, he'd have agreed with her.

"I thought you said that it was better to let them flounder on their own for a day or two," Uless remarked.

Matt took note of Uless's considering look. Because of his back-to-back appointments, he hadn't had the opportunity to explain the scene between him and Doria that the young man had witnessed.

"Uless, about what you saw this morning . . ."

Uless held up his hand. "Look, Matt, what's going on between you and the lady treasury agent is your business. My lip is zipped."

"There's nothing going on between us!" Matt said in exasperation.

"Whatever you say." Uless glanced at his watch. "If you're going to ask her to lunch, you'd better get a move on. There's only one decent restaurant around here, and it will be packed in fifteen minutes. It's bad form to keep a hungry lady waiting."

Matt grumbled to himself about wisecracking punks as he headed for Doria's office. She was so absorbed in what she was doing that she didn't see him. Matt took advantage of the opportunity to observe her.

Her face was screwed up in concentration. She used to wear a similar expression when she was getting ready to steal something from the corner grocery while he distracted Old Man Baron, the owner. He recalled how he'd once gotten on his macho high-horse, insisting that she do the distracting and let him cop the food. She'd objected strenuously, claiming that the shopkeepers always suspected boys of being up to no good, so she had a better chance of getting away with it. And she had always gotten away with it, though Matt now suspected that Baron had known exactly what was going on and chose to ignore it.

He pulled himself away from the past and knocked on the door. When Doria looked up in surprise, he said, "It's almost noon. How about joining me for lunch? It'll be Dutch, of course. I'd never want to be accused of trying to bribe a treasury agent."

Doria had to swallow against the sudden lump in her throat. Matt looked so sexy standing in the doorway with his thumbs hooked in his belt loops and his hands splayed over his abdomen, drawing her attention to his zipper. Her mind immediately conjured up images of elephants and giraffes, and she glanced up quickly, but not quickly enough. The insolent twist to Matt's lips told her that he was aware of where she'd been looking.

Her common sense told her to turn down his invitation, but she needed to talk to him about a truce. The faster she got him off her back, the faster she'd get this job done. Then they could both get on with their lives, and the past could be relegated to nothing more than a bad memory.

She exited from her computer program, dug her wallet out of her briefcase and rose to her feet. "Lunch sounds great, but please choose a place with a moderate price range. Treasury agents don't make the big bucks that you CPA's do."

*"Big bucks?"* Matt repeated, theatrically bringing his hands to his chest. "Don't I wish. The big firms make the big bucks. Us little guys barely survive."

Doria knew he was exaggerating. He might not be dripping in money, but her contacts had assured her that he wasn't hurting. "In that case, am I going to pick out the fast-food joint, or are you? I don't want to put a crimp in your budget."

"I can afford more than a burger."

The street was crowded when they left the building. They strolled along in a surprisingly companionable silence. It had been a long time since Doria had felt this relaxed with anyone. In fact, she probably hadn't felt this way since before Matt had been bundled off to Colorado. It wasn't because she hadn't met a lot of nice men over the years, because she had. A couple of them had even been special. But when they'd begun to press for a commitment, she'd turned tail and run.

She wasn't adverse to commitment as much as she was adverse to a relationship that wasn't based on truth. By the time she got deep enough into a relationship to realize it had potential, she'd already taken the man on a journey through her mythical childhood.

"Hey, we're here," Matt said.

"Sorry. I guess my mind was elsewhere."

"If that's a backhanded compliment about my stimulating company, I'm insulted," he complained mildly.

It was the easy repartee they'd used to share, and she grinned at him. "Don't worry about it. You have other admirable traits to compensate for your boredom."

"You're as smart-mouthed as ever," he accused with a chuckle.

After they were seated and both had ordered salads, Doria asked, "What happened to your parents? They moved shortly after you left, and no one knew where they'd gone."

She regretted the question when Matt's expression turned hard. Several tension-filled seconds passed. Just when she was convinced he wasn't going to answer, he said, "Dad's emphysema got worse, and the doctors told him to get out of L.A. Dan—that's Mom's cousin who took me in—gave them the money to move to Arizona. Dad died a year later."

"I'm so sorry," Doria said with heartfelt sympathy. She'd liked Matt's father, whose illness had incapacitated him at a young age. His disability pension had been no more than a pittance, and since he'd required constant care, Matt's mother had been unable to work. In order for them to survive, they'd been forced to move into the old neighborhood when Matt was a toddler.

"I don't want your condolences," Matt stated, his gaze condemning. "Because of you, I wasn't with my father when he died. I didn't even get to tell him goodbye."

Doria closed her eyes to protect herself against the pain that surged through her at his indictment. She now understood why Matt hadn't forgiven her. Though he'd fought with his father constantly, she'd never doubted that he loved him. Unlike her, Matt hadn't been as much a rebel as he'd been rebellious. He'd been intelligent, inquisitive and bored. To counteract that boredom, he'd sought excitement. When he'd hooked up with her, she'd supplied him with plenty of it, because she'd been on a downward spiral toward disaster.

Oddly enough, it was Matt's being sent away that had straightened her out. It made her angry. Angry at him for leaving. Angry at herself for causing his departure. Angry at the world in general, because she hadn't thought it was fair that Matt should get out of the ghetto and she should have to stay behind.

That anger could have had a negative effect, but it had made her determined. She'd decided that if Matt could get out, so could she. She'd started going to school regularly. She'd started living at the library and reading voraciously. She'd even started working part-time for Old Man Baron at the corner grocery instead of robbing him twice a week.

Three years later, her efforts had paid off. She'd been accepted into college, and she'd walked out of the old neighborhood and never looked back.

Until now. And though she hated Matt's damning expression, she found the courage to look him squarely in the eye. "I know that saying I'm sorry isn't much compensation. If I could go back and change everything, I would. Unfortunately I can't, and since I can't, why can't we declare a truce until Halliford's audit is over?

"As soon as it's done, I'll walk out of your life, and you'll never see me again," she continued before he could respond. "I'd do that now, but we're shorthanded at the office. There isn't anyone else to do the audit."

Matt felt torn by her words. He wanted to hang on to the anger he felt toward her, but it was being chased away by an emotion that felt like alarm. It took him a moment to realize that it was because Doria was saying she would walk out of his life and he'd never see her again. He should have been elated, but he wasn't.

He reached into his pocket for a cigarette, cursing when he didn't find one. He couldn't think rationally when he wasn't smoking. His jacket pocket was stuffed with sunflower seeds, but he wouldn't eat them in front of Doria any more than he would Uless. It would be a sign of his indecision, and he wasn't about to make himself that vulnerable. She looked sincerely remorseful, but could he trust her? If he could, did he want to? He didn't know, but until he did, he wasn't ready to close the doors.

He extended his hand across the table. "Truce."

Doria let out a sigh of relief as she accepted it. They fell back into silence and though she knew she could be stepping into another minefield, she felt compelled to ask, "What happened to your mother?"

He smiled, and Doria was entranced. It was the first true smile she'd seen on his face since she'd walked back into his life. She'd forgotten how nice it was.

"She's doing great. She remarried, and Bill thinks the sun rises and sets on her. They have a big ranch in Arizona, and it's like pulling teeth to get her away from it."

"It must be a wonderful place."

"It is." He folded his arms on the table and stared wistfully off into the distance. "Someday I hope to have a place just like it, though I don't think I'll choose the desert. It's too barren for me. But wherever it is, it'll be wide-open spaces. A perfect place to raise a family."

His statement sparked a deep longing inside Doria. She'd entertained similar fantasies since childhood, but they were as far from her grasp now as they'd been then.

It was so depressing that she would have sunk into a blue funk if the waitress hadn't chosen that moment to deliver their meal. The food seemed to cheer Matt, too, because he visibly relaxed.

After they'd coated their salads with dressing, he casually asked, "So, what do you think of Halliford?"

Doria bit her lip to stop her grin when she recalled Matt's complimentary underwear. She was tempted to tease him about it, but knew better. She'd have to work with Matt for several weeks. During that time she'd be challenging him. At some point, he might take it as a personal affront. Her little weapon could prove to be handy.

"It wouldn't be prudent for me to discuss their case at this point. I've barely had a chance to look at their records."

He muttered what sounded like a curse, and a rather imaginative one at that. "Don't pretend to be obtuse, Doria. That isn't what I was asking, and you know it."

"Well, what, exactly, were you asking?" she responded with a look of wide-eyed naiveté.

"Don't pull that innocent act with me. I know you, remember?"

Doria's insides scrambled. He did know her. In ways that no other man could. She suddenly realized that this was why she'd never been able to tell the truth to the special men in her life. She could never describe in words what her existence had been like. She could never have given them the texture, and without it they could have never understood. With Matt, she didn't have to explain. He'd been there.

"I was a bit surprised to find out they were your client," she confessed. "They're so reminiscent of our past."

Matt's eyes danced with devilry. "That's exactly why I took them on. One of my fondest memories was sneaking into Sal's strip joint. Best class I ever had on female anatomy."

"Matt!" Doria exclaimed in mock chastisement. "You should be ashamed of yourself."

"Don't be ridiculous, Doria. A boy has to get his sex education somewhere."

"As I recall, your collection of *Playboy* magazines was quite extensive."

"Sure, but it was one-dimensional. It didn't give me that good sense of shake, rattle and roll."

Why was she blushing? Because Matt's gaze had strayed to her breasts during his last statement?

She concentrated on her salad as she said, "Well, I'm sure that you've learned that there is more to a woman than her, uh, assets."

Matt chuckled in delight. "Is that what they're called now? Assets?"

"Matthew Peter Cutter, you're being rude."

"And you're blushing. Why?"

"Because this isn't the type of conversation you have in public," she stated primly.

"Why not? There's nothing wrong with the human body."

"I know that, but . . ."

"But?"

She scowled at him. "You're purposely tormenting me, so stop it. We declared a truce, remember?"

"Our truce had nothing to do with Halliford."

"We aren't talking about Halliford."

"Sure, we are. Halliford deals in sex, and the world revolves around sex."

"That's so sexist, it turns my stomach," Doria muttered. She pointed her fork at him. "How would you like it if you were judged on your assets?"

His smile was pure male arrogance. "I haven't had any complaints."

"That's male drivel of the first order," she jeered. "A man drops his drawers and expects a woman to swoon. Well, I hate to burst your bubble, but ninety-nine out of a hundred times, she's faking it."

"Really?" Matt murmured in mock amazement. "Are you telling me that if I stood up and dropped my pants, most of the women in here wouldn't faint?"

"Oh, they'd faint, all right, but it wouldn't be out of admiration."

"And how do you know that? From what I hear, those male exotic dancers make a bundle. All those sex-crazed women stuff money down their pants. You can't tell me that a lot of them aren't trying to cop a feel."

"Matt!" Doria scolded when a few people glanced toward them. "We're sitting in a restaurant, so stop it. I agreed to have lunch with you. I didn't agree to make a spectacle of myself."

"Would making a spectacle of yourself bother you?"

"Of course, it would. I'm a treasury agent. I have an image to uphold." Uneasy with the avid way he was staring at her, she glanced at her watch. "It's time for me to get back to the office. You may be able to indulge in long lunch-hours, but I work for Uncle Sam. He says that I'm only entitled to one hour."

Matt signaled for their checks. "And who's going to tell him if you take an extra five minutes?"

"Probably no one, but I'd know I was breaking the rules, and I'd be terribly disappointed in myself."

Matt was unsettled by her answer. The old Doria wouldn't have cared about the rules. She would have done what she wanted and damn the consequences. Plus, she wouldn't have been so concerned about image. How could she exist in a world that told her how to behave? How to live?

He wasn't being fair, he told himself when they left the restaurant. The old Doria had been a fourteen-year-old kid. Today she was a responsible woman. He'd be disappointed if she hadn't changed. So why was he disappointed that she had?

The question deviled him all the way back to the office. He was forced to put it aside when Uless handed him a stack of messages and turned the phone over to him while he went to lunch.

He should hire an answering service, or at least invest in an answering machine, Matt thought irritably when the phone began to ring off the hook. He didn't want to be bothered by clients. He needed to think. Uless's lunch hour turned into an hour and a half, and worse, Uless didn't even offer Matt a "Sorry I'm late" when he returned. Maybe he should take a lesson from Uncle Sam, Matt thought with irritation.

Rather than giving in to the urge to growl at Uless, Matt went into his office and closed the door. He'd never believed in punching a time clock. If Uless took a few extra minutes, he always made up for them. What was wrong with him?

Unfortunately the answer to that question was all too evident—Doria Sinclair.

As he sat with his back to his desk and stared out the window, he told himself that Doria's transformation had been inevitable. He'd changed, too, hadn't he? Of course he had, but not so drastically. He'd mellowed, while Doria had done a complete about-face.

He had the feeling she was running, but he didn't know from what and to where. All he knew was that he kept hearing her say, *I know that saying I'm sorry isn't much compensation. If I could go back and change everything, I would.*

Her actions had cost him the last days with his father, but what would it have cost her? Her father? Maybe. But would that have been so bad? Again, maybe. Matt's work in the ghetto had shown him that the most abused children were often the most devoted to their parents. It didn't make sense, but it was a fact of life. He'd learned not to question the facts of life. All he could do was be there for them, but his competition was fierce.

When he and Doria had grown up, there'd been drugs. There'd been gangs, and there'd been social diseases. Through some miracle, they'd managed to avoid all three. But today, there weren't just drugs, there were crack houses, and once they'd lured you through the door, it was nearly impossible to get you back. The gangs of his and Doria's youth were mean, but they hadn't carried Saturday night specials that had a better chance of blowing up in your face and killing you than the target you were aiming at. There also hadn't been AIDS, which was in epidemic proportions. Even free handouts of condoms weren't helping. Half the people were so zonked-out on drugs that they couldn't remember to use protection if they wanted to. The worst victims of it all were the babies born as junkies or infected with AIDS.

Matt, along with a group of professional men and women who'd all come off the streets, were fighting the war in the only way they knew how. It was a one-on-one battle. With any luck, each of them managed to save a kid like Uless once a year. Hopefully the Ulesses would each save a kid, and eventually the war would be won.

But what about the Doria Sinclairs of the world? No one had been there to save them. If it hadn't been for his cousin, Matt suspected he'd never have made it out. However, Doria had, and she'd lost something when she'd made the transition. And that something was her identity. Could he help her find it? Or had she become so inured against the past that she'd remain a lost soul forever?

Matt knew he had to try to reach her. For a time he, too, had lost his identity, and he'd never been so miserable in his life. Despite his ambivalence toward Doria—or maybe because of it—he couldn't bear the thought of her living the rest of her life in misery.

DORIA LOOKED UP when Matt swaggered into her office, his hands stuffed into his pants pockets and his lips curved into a Cheshire-cat grin.

"How's it going?" he asked.

"Not bad," Doria answered. "You and Halliford have kept good records. I have a few questions that we can discuss later, but I haven't come across any serious problems. Of course, I'm just beginning, so you're not off the hook yet."

He chuckled as he sat on the edge of her desk. Doria gulped as her eyes dropped to his bunched thigh. How could such a skinny kid have turned out to be such a muscular man?

"Well, you can worry about hooking me tomorrow. Right now, my stomach says it's time for dinner."

"Dinner?" Doria parroted as she tugged her eyes away from his leg and glanced at her watch. "It's only a quarter to four."

Matt leaned forward and lifted her wrist. Doria's pulse went from zero to sixty in two seconds flat.

He clucked sympathetically and shook his head. "That's what you get for depending on a watch that runs on a battery. I have one of those old-fashioned ones that you wind every morning. It never goes dead. It's almost six-thirty, Doria. Uless left an hour ago."

"Six-thirty?" she repeated breathlessly. He was brushing his thumb against the inside of her wrist, and her pulse was getting ready to switch into warp drive. "But it can't be six-thirty."

"It's amazing how fast time flies when you're having fun."

His grin was so infectious that Doria couldn't help laughing. "You're impossible."

"Starving is a better description. How about dinner?"

Doria shook her head. "I can't Matt, and you know it. I'm a treasury agent auditing your client. It's against the rules."

"If someone sees us, you can introduce me as an old friend. Who's going to know the difference?"

"I'd know."

"What if I promise that I won't even mention Halliford?"

"Matt, I can't. I could lose my job if someone saw us together. Even if it's innocent, it isn't innocent if people think it isn't."

"I could tape our conversation."

"Matt!" she wailed in frustration.

"What if we went somewhere where no one could see us? Would you have dinner with me then?"

"There isn't such a place."

"Of course, there is."

Doria eyed him suspiciously. "And where, pray tell, is that?"

"Your place or mine."

"No." He was already making her pulse race. She wasn't going to get stuck in the intimacy of one of their homes so he could make her heart pound. Matt turned her on, but he also loathed her, and though they'd made a truce, she didn't trust him to uphold it outside the office.

"Why not? Didn't you make your bed this morning?" he asked with a leering grin.

"Did you?" she shot back.

He lowered his voice to a sexy rasp. "No. I happen to like a rumpled bed. It looks . . . friendly, if you know what I mean."

Unfortunately, she did, and her heart was pounding hard enough without the stimulus of an intimate atmosphere.

Maybe Halliford's records were the problem, she thought, eager at this point to grasp at any straw. She'd spent so much time today reading about and looking at pictures of naughty novelty underwear and costumes, that her hormones had gotten all stirred up. It didn't have anything to do with Matt, and if she just pictured him in one of those ridiculous animal jockstraps, everything would return to normal.

The exercise might have worked if Matt hadn't chosen that moment to stand, putting her at eye level with his zipper. She glanced away quickly and cursed silently when she felt a blush crawl into her cheeks.

*Just stop it!* she scolded herself. *Good heavens, you didn't look long enough to get a good impression, so you don't have any reason to be embarrassed.*

"Come on, Doria," Matt cajoled. "I hate to eat alone, and we've declared a truce. It'll be a friendly dinner between two old friends. We won't discuss business. I promise, and you know I never break a promise."

Doria did know that. The trouble was, it wasn't discussing business that she was worried about. It was the effect Matt was having on her, and the fear that if she said yes, she'd be opening a Pandora's box.

She told herself she'd say no. She *promised* herself she'd say no. Being friendly with Matt on the job was one thing. Being friendly with him off the job was quite another. It could destroy her squeaky-clean reputation and cost her her job. That might be exactly what Matt wanted to happen. She didn't want to believe he'd be that vindictive, but she couldn't afford to discount the possibility.

"Well?" he prodded when she remained silent.

Again, Doria told herself to say no. When she opened her mouth, however, what came out was, "It'll have to be at your place. I haven't been shopping and my cupboards are bare."

"Great. My place it is," he said triumphantly. "Grab your computer and briefcase, and let's hit the road."

*It'll be okay,* she assured her conscience when it began to hyperventilate. *It'll be at his place with my car, so if things get sticky, I can run like hell.*

To her chagrin, her conscience was quick to remind her that she'd left her running shoes at home, tucked beneath her unmade bed, which looked friendly as all get out as she stared at Matt's retreating backside.

# 4

DORIA WASN'T SURPRISED when she learned that Matt drove a motorcycle, so she didn't know why she was startled when she saw where he lived. The old, two-story frame house was badly in need of a paint job and was located in the same rundown neighborhood as his office. The house couldn't actually be described as a dump, but it was close enough to one to make her feel uncomfortable. Why would Matt choose to live like this when he didn't have to?

She watched him climb off his motorcycle and remove his helmet. He tucked it beneath his arm and walked toward her car with an unconscious swagger that automatically drew her gaze to his narrow hips. Good heavens, why was she so obsessed with his zipper?

It was those darn jockstraps, she thought disgruntledly. If she had one iota of common sense, she'd head for home. Matt was touching her on a sexual level. Even if he shared that attraction, he despised her, which meant that if he acted on those feelings, he'd end up despising himself.

She couldn't let that happen. She'd seen firsthand what self-loathing could do to a person. Following her mother's death she'd watched it eat at her father until he'd finally struck out at her. When that hadn't eased his torment, he'd turned his hatred back on himself. If there was even a remote chance that Matt might be attracted to her, she had to get out of here.

She reached for the key, but drew her hand back. It had been her experience that men like Matt had some egotistical need to pursue the unobtainable woman. If she truly wanted to keep her distance, she had to stay. With a resolved sigh, she climbed out of her car, wishing with all her heart that she could be anyplace in the world but here. Well, anyplace but here or the old neighborhood, she quickly amended.

Matt eyed Doria curiously when she got out of her car. Her expression was one of cool haughtiness, which meant she felt threatened. When he drew close enough to see the wariness in her eyes, he had the distinct impression that she felt threatened by him.

And maybe she should feel that way, he concluded when his eyes roamed over her. She'd put in a long day, but she looked as perfectly groomed as she had when she'd first walked into the office. His body stirred with the tempting thought of mussing her up from head to toe, and he stopped at the front of her white Ford compact, leaning a hip against its fender. He'd be flirting with fire if he got any closer.

"Welcome to my humble abode," he said.

"Yeah." Doria glanced up and down the seedy street. "Will my car be safe here?"

So that was it! She wasn't afraid of him. She was afraid of the neighborhood. But why? She might look as if she couldn't fight her way out of a wet paper bag, but he knew it would be unwise to underestimate her. She had once been the dirtiest street fighter he'd ever met.

"Your car is probably safer here than in a police impound. We have a unique neighborhood-watch program."

"How's it unique?"

He gave a nonchalant shrug. "The Sinners are my friends."

Doria gaped as he levered himself away from her car and walked toward his house. The Sinners had been one of the most fearsome gangs in Los Angeles when she and Matt were growing up. And Matt was *connected* with them?

Again, Doria's instincts told her to hightail it out of there, but curiosity and concern made her follow him. Matt had everything going for him. If he was risking his future by involving himself with the Sinners, wasn't she obligated to make him see the error of his ways?

Matt was waiting for her at the door. When he gestured for her to precede him, Doria stepped inside, coming to an abrupt halt at the chaos that greeted her. Half the ceiling of the small foyer was ripped out. So were the walls, exposing electrical wiring and wooden beams that looked as if they suffered from termite damage. Lumber and building materials were stacked to one side, and she nearly stumbled over a pile of paint cans when she walked farther into the house.

"Excuse the mess," Matt said. "I'm remodeling."

"Are you sure you aren't demolishing?" Doria responded as she gawked at her surroundings. She'd seen condemned buildings in better shape than this.

Matt chuckled. "I guess I'm doing that, too. Walk straight ahead and you'll find the kitchen."

Doria cast surreptitious glances into the shadowed rooms they passed. What little furniture they contained was covered with sheets, and each successive room seemed to be in even more disrepair than the last.

When she walked through the swing doors leading into the kitchen, she was flooded with relief. The walls needed to be painted and the wood cabinets were in various stages of being refinished, but at least it wasn't torn apart. As she sank onto a chair at the old oak table, she was hit with the understanding of how orderly her own life was. She'd go crazy if she had to face this mess every day.

"How long have you been remodeling?" she asked as Matt dropped his motorcycle helmet onto the table, shed his leather jacket and hung it across the back of a chair. He then crossed to the refrigerator, pulled out two beers and tossed her one without bothering to ask if she wanted it. Doria was irritated by his impoliteness. She considered refusing the drink, but she liked beer and rarely drank it. Wine was the preferred libation among the crowd she socialized with. She popped open the tab and took a sip.

"A little over a year now." Matt leaned against the sink and took a hefty gulp from his can. "I'm using mostly local labor, so it's taking a bit longer than normal."

"By local labor, you mean ghetto labor," she said.

Matt shrugged. "I mean labor that can use the money. Unemployment is a major problem around here."

"Your decision to hire the unemployed is commendable, but wouldn't you be better off hiring a contractor and getting the work done quickly?"

"If I hired a contractor, I wouldn't be in control of the project."

"The control is what appeals to you, isn't it?"

"And control doesn't appeal to you?" he countered with a sardonic smile. "Come on, Doria, you don't work for the IRS for altruistic reasons. You work for them because it gives you a sense of power. You want control as much as I do."

"That's not true," Doria said defensively. "I work for the IRS because it's a secure job. I'd be willing to bet that you became a CPA for the same reason. It's a career that gives you a chance to be your own boss, but if it doesn't work out, there are plenty of opportunities to work for someone else. You made that career choice because you no longer wanted to fight for survival. You made it because you wanted security as much as I did."

"When I first set out to become a CPA, I may have been looking for security," Matt admitted. "I soon discovered, however, that it wasn't worth the price. I was expected to conform to a set of standards I didn't believe in. When I refused to conform, I was ostracized."

Doria released a disbelieving laugh as she glanced pointedly at the torn knee in his denims. "You still aren't conforming, but you're accepted. You've built one hell of a reputation for yourself."

"I have built one hell of a reputation for myself," he agreed. "And my clients turn both their personal and business records over to me without blinking an eye. But how do you think they'd react if I wanted to date their daughters?"

"If you played the role of successful businessman, they wouldn't blink an eye over that, either," Doria noted dryly. "But instead of playing the role, you dress like an aging juvenile delinquent. Your office looks like a cross between *Good Housekeeping* and bad taste. Then there's your secretary."

"What's wrong with Uless?" he asked so softly that Doria realized she was treading on shaky ground.

"Nothing's wrong with Uless that a little social polishing wouldn't cure. He looks like a hood, Matt, and a very dangerous one, at that."

"He *is* a hood," Matt said. "I'm a hood, and no amount of social polishing is going to change that. We can rise above our circumstances, Doria, but we can never completely shed our past."

"That's not true!" Doria exclaimed as she unconsciously sprang to her feet and tapped her index finger against her chest. "Look at me."

Matt's gaze flicked over her disparagingly. "Yes, look at you. Your designer labels alone declare that you're the epitome of success, but what has it gotten you?"

"A decent place to live, food on the table, and money in the bank," she answered fiercely.

"I'll grant you that all those things are important, but be honest with yourself, Doria. You may be surviving in more comfort than you did when you were a kid, but I'd bet that you're more alone today than you were fourteen years ago."

Matt's words slashed through Doria with the ease of a finely honed knife-blade. She couldn't believe that he'd be so cruel as to attack her with the very confession she'd made to him as a girl. She'd told him that if it wasn't for him, she'd be completely alone, and that that frightened her. He'd told her that her fear was unnecessary, that he'd always be there for her. Then he'd gone away, fulfilling her worst nightmare.

"You don't know what you're talking about," she stated disdainfully. Her pride would never allow her to reveal how much he'd hurt her. "I have more friends than I can count."

"Friends or acquaintances?" Matt challenged.

Doria wanted to proclaim that all her friends were friends, but they were nothing more than acquaintances. She had to keep them at arm's length. If she let them get too close, they might learn the truth, and she had a deep-seated fear that what Matt had said was true. No amount of social polishing could change what she was. That concept was so terrifying that she refused to face it. She also knew that she had to get away from Matt before she said or did something she'd end up regretting.

Thankfully, her briefcase and computer were in the trunk of her car. Her keys were in her jacket pocket. She could walk out on him with dignity. She strode toward the swing doors without so much as a backward glance. The first thing in the morning she would persuade Dryer to take her off the Halliford audit, even if she had to come up with still another lie.

Matt cursed lowly when Doria walked out with all the regal bearing of a queen. Her posture alone told him how much he'd hurt her, and he felt ashamed. Even if his assumption about her life was true, to taunt her with her aloneness was cruel. Admitting he owed her an apology, Matt headed after her.

"Doria, please wait. We need to talk," he urged, exiting the kitchen.

Doria rounded on him, her eyes flashing with anger. "What we *need* is to stay away from each other. All we've done for the past two days is sling arrows at one another, and I surrender.

"You're right, Matt," she continued without even pausing for breath. "I'm the lowest form of person who's ever walked the face of the earth. So I'm going to slink back to my comfortable, albeit lonely, apartment and wallow in my sins. Will that give you enough satisfaction? Or should I pick up a whip on the way home and strip a few pounds of flesh off my designer-label hide?"

"Dammit, Doria, stop being melodramatic," Matt muttered as he stuffed his hands into his pockets and rocked back on his heels.

"You're accusing me of being melodramatic?" she gasped in outrage. "Take a look around you, Matt. When you're done doing that, look at yourself in the mirror. You may not like what I've become, but at least I've grown up!" With that, she resumed her march toward the door.

Matt's temper erupted with volcanic force. A moment ago he'd been ready to apologize for hurting her feelings. Now he wanted to wring her neck! How dare she accuse him of being childish!

He caught up with her in two strides, grabbed her arm and spun her around. He was so furious that he didn't see the look of utter fear that settled on her face. But what his eyes didn't see, his heart heard when she let out a strangled yelp of terror. He was so stunned by the sound that he could only stare down at her. When her expression did register, he was jolted to the depths of his soul. She honestly thought he could hurt her!

He knew that the best way to reassure her was to release her, but he couldn't bring himself to do so. If she bolted before he convinced her he'd never harm her, she'd always be afraid of him. He'd never be able to live with that.

He raised a hand and threaded his fingers into her hair, gently cupping the back of her head. Instead of the action soothing her as he'd intended, her eyes widened even farther in distress. As his mind groped for the words to comfort her, he automatically drew her closer. When she trembled as their bodies touched, he suddenly understood that it wasn't words she needed, but a more basic kind of reassurance. He lowered his head and brushed his lips across hers.

The moment Matt grabbed Doria and she saw the fury reflected in his face, all the fear that she'd thought long ago buried flooded to the surface. Her survival instincts instantly kicked into gear, telling her not to move. Any action on her part would provoke a violent reaction. Nevertheless, she was unable to stop the small cry of fear from surfacing when he hauled her up against him.

As she stared up at him, his visage wavered and splintered until it was her father before her. The hatred in his eyes was so absolute that it seared through her, hurting her far more deeply than any blow he could deliver. In defense, her mind began to search for that elusive black hole to oblivion. If she could find it, she could crawl into it and never have to come out. She'd never have to look into her father's accusing eyes again. She'd never—

Her frantic thoughts were brought to a jarring halt when something warm and soft brushed across her lips. It was in such acute contrast to the pain she'd been anticipating that she stiffened in shock. It was only when Matt brushed his lips across hers a second time that reality began to set in. She wasn't facing her father. This was Matt, and though he had a temper, he was not violent. So why had she flipped out like that?

She wanted to think the question through, but her mind kept short-circuiting and zinging its way back to the tantalizing brush of Matt's lips. To the warmth of his body as it pressed against hers. To the reassurance of his strong arms cradling her. When he finally pressed his lips firmly to hers, Doria could no longer remember the question, because it required all her concentration just to remain standing.

Some little voice inside began to nag at her, telling her this was wrong, but she thrust it aside. It might be wrong, but she'd been alone for so long and yearned for what Matt was offering. She wrapped her arms around his neck and parted her lips.

Matt answered her invitation with a low, guttural groan. Doria's head began to reel as he crushed her against him and plunged his tongue into her mouth. It was the most ravishing kiss Doria had ever experienced, and she burrowed even more closely against him, silently begging him for more.

Matt gave her what she sought. Then he teased her by withdrawing his tongue slowly, forcing her to follow his thrust and parry, until she was the one doing the ravishing. Desire rushed through her when his entire body shuddered as her tongue dueled feverishly with his.

Suddenly he grasped her hips and ground his pelvis urgently against hers. She'd been vaguely aware of his growing arousal, but the proof of just how aroused he was was as startling to her as it was electrifying. It also snapped her back to reality. She jerked away from the kiss and leaped backward. Heaven help her, what was she doing?

"I'm sorry, Matt," Doria whispered hoarsely when he stared at her in dazed bafflement, "but we can't do this. I'm auditing your client, remember?"

Matt's first thought was that she was joking, but her sober expression assured him she was serious. He couldn't believe it! He was more turned-on than he'd been in years, and she was worried about professional mores?

He knew he was being crude, but he gestured toward the front of his pants saying, "I understand that fooling around with me might go against your professional standards, but what in hell am I supposed to do with this?"

Doria blushed and ducked her head, unable to meet his frustrated gaze. "I believe the standard remedy is a cold shower."

"That's a typical female response," he drawled with heavy sarcasm. "A woman gets a man all hot and bothered, and then tells him to take a cold shower. Well, I hate to be the one to break this to you, but that cure is highly overrated."

"I'm sorry," Doria repeated, her blush deepening. "I never meant for anything like this to happen. When it started I should have put a stop to it. I should have—"

"Stop playing the martyr," Matt interrupted impatiently, unable to decide if he was irritated by her meek contriteness or with himself for kissing her in the first place. "I was as much a participant as you were."

She glanced up at him in relief. "Then it's okay."

"I didn't say that," he grumbled, plowing his hand through his hair. In fact, he wasn't sure he'd ever be okay again. The reality of kissing Doria had far exceeded any fantasy he'd dreamed up. Hell, who was he trying to kid?

It had far exceeded any reality he'd experienced. If she was that good at kissing, what would she be like in bed? He groaned inwardly at the thought.

"Well, I guess I should be going," Doria said, nervously edging her way toward the door.

"You're not going anywhere until you've eaten," Matt murmured.

"I don't think that's a good idea," Doria demurred.

Matt's temper began to stir, but he forced himself to remain calm. "Look, Doria, I may not be the three-piece-suit, hotshot type you're used to dealing with, but I do have enough savoir faire to know that when a woman says no, she means no. Now, I'm going to feed you dinner, and that's final."

Doria opened her mouth to object, but closed it when she saw the determined glint in his eyes. To oppose him at this point would only cause another confrontation, and she'd just learned how he handled confrontations. She wasn't sure she'd be strong enough to say no if they ended up in another clinch.

"All right. I'll stay for dinner," she acquiesced reluctantly.

MATT EYED DORIA as he prepared spaghetti and garlic bread. She'd insisted on helping with dinner, so he'd let her make the salad. She was working with quiet concentration, and he wondered if she was thinking about the kiss they'd shared.

He had his own conflicting feelings about the kiss. The logical side of his nature insisted that it had been a mistake. The male side, however, was speculating on whether a repeat performance would be as powerful a turn-on. There was only one way to find out, but what would he do if a second kiss was as good? Even if he could overcome his grievances against her, Doria had changed. Matt suspected that the differences between them were too great to overcome.

Doria was excruciatingly aware of Matt's attention as she sliced vegetables. She ignored him, but she couldn't disregard the tumultuous feelings roiling inside her. To combat them, she went over all the reasons why she couldn't get involved with him. Her mind applauded her fortitude, but her libido scoffed at her.

She jumped when Matt came up behind her and said, "Watch your head. I need to get the plates."

Doria gulped when he opened the cupboard door and leaned close enough for her to feel his body heat. She couldn't decide if she wanted to flee or throw herself into his arms. She opted to engage him in conversation, instead.

When he carried the plates to the table, she asked, "What's your connection with the Sinners?"

"I told you. We're friends."

"You used to hate gangs."

"I still hate them."

"So, why align yourself with them?"

He retrieved silverware from a nearby drawer and returned to the table. "I'm not aligning myself with them. I'm using them to my advantage."

"You're arguing semantics, Matt."

He grinned devilishly. "Yeah, I guess I am."

"This is not a laughing matter," Doria grumbled. "You've made something of yourself, and you're endangering all your hard work by becoming involved with the Sinners."

"In other words, I have an image to uphold."

"Exactly."

"Well, Doria, this may come as a shock, but I don't give a flip about image."

"Even if that's true, how could you hang around with a gang?"

He put the last of the silverware on the table and propped a hand on his hip. "I don't hang around with the Sinners. I hire them to do odd jobs. In return, they help keep an eye on my neighborhood."

"You'd be better off moving into a safer neighborhood," Doria observed. "You know as well as I do that you can't trust a gang. They're like pit bulls. They'll turn on you at the slightest provocation."

"They're human beings, not animals," Matt said in exasperation. "And deep down, most of them are decent kids growing up in a world that strips them of their dignity. Polite society ignores them, because the problem is so vast that it seems insurmountable. The leeches of society feed off them, taking what little they do have and turning them into junkies and prostitutes. They're confused and frightened and angry, and they band together in an effort to survive. You, of all people, should understand that."

"Why should I understand it?" Doria questioned derisively. "You and I grew up in that world, but we never developed the gang mentality."

"Are you sure about that?" Matt crossed his arms over his chest and gave her a grim smile. "You and I weren't part of an official gang, but that's because we'd formed our own gang. The only difference between us was numbers."

Doria gazed at him in disbelief. "You have to be joking. The difference between us was that they were violent."

"Our modus operandi was different, but our motivation was fundamentally the same."

Not willing to accept that Matt was right, Doria frowned. She dismissed his premise and said, "That still doesn't explain why you're associating with the Sinners. They're known for their violence, and I can't believe you condone that."

"I don't condone it, but you have to prove to a street kid that it's more productive to use his brains than his brawn. You have to teach him the value of an education and convince him that it will get him out of the ghetto for good."

"You're talking about Uless, aren't you?" Doria asked thoughtfully, recalling that the young man went to school three afternoons a week. "Was he a member of the Sinners?"

"He's their leader."

Doria's jaw dropped. "Your secretary is a gang leader? Are you crazy?"

"Like a fox," Matt answered smugly. "If you can turn the leader around, then the rest of the gang is bound to follow suit. Before you know it, they'll all be in school learning a vocation."

Doria gave a flabbergasted shake of her head. He might think he was crazy like a fox, but she thought he was nuts!

"Matt, what you're saying is wonderful in theory, but you can't be naive enough to expect it to work. And have you considered the consequences if it doesn't? By exposing Uless to your clients' personal tax records you're providing him with a virtual smorgasbord of people to rob. Good heavens, he can pick out the most promising marks by simply making note of their gross income. He can discern which homes will be empty during the day by noting whether both a husband and wife work. You might as well rent a van and back it up to their front doors yourself!"

"Uless isn't going to rob my clients," Matt stated confidently as the timer for the spaghetti went off. He walked to the stove and removed it. "It will only take a couple of minutes to heat the sauce, so you'd better finish the salad."

Doria didn't know what to say. There was only one way that Matt could be so certain of Uless's loyalty. He had to have done something to make Uless feel as if he owed him. A shiver crawled up her spine. Whatever it was had to have been dangerous. Bravery was the only act the Sinners admired.

She studied Matt as he retrieved the garlic bread from the oven. Up to this point, she'd considered him a harmless, respectable hoodlum, but even as a boy he hadn't been harmless. When you grew up on the streets, you learned quickly how to take care of yourself. It was a matter of survival.

She was so busy concentrating on Matt that she wasn't paying attention to what she was doing. She let out a yelp of surprise when she sliced through a cauliflower floret and nicked her finger.

"What's wrong?" Matt asked, appearing instantly at her side. "Damn, you've cut your finger." He hauled her over to the sink, turned on the cold water and stuck her hand beneath it.

"Matt, it's just a scratch," Doria muttered, uncomfortable with his solicitousness.

"Scratches don't gush."

"It's not gushing. It's—"

"Doria, for once, don't be argumentative," he interrupted impatiently.

"I'm not being argumentative. I'm . . ."

Matt caught her chin and tilted her face up to his. "What do I have to do to shut you up? Kiss you?"

The gravelly edge to his voice and the provocative gleam in his eyes sent a rush of desire through Doria so intense she couldn't speak. She knew she couldn't let him kiss her again, but oh, how she wished she could!

Matt gave a wry laugh. "I guess the threat is enough to render you mute. Let's take care of your finger."

Doria knew it was a superficial cut, but his gentle ministrations made her melancholy. The last person to show her this much caring had been her mother, and she'd died when Doria was eight.

"Am I hurting you?" Matt asked when he noted Doria's odd expression.

Doria shook her head. "I was just recalling how you used to turn green at the sight of blood."

She was surprised when his cheeks reddened. He shut off the water, grabbed a paper towel and dried her hand. "Well, between you and me, it still makes me queasy. Keep pressure on the cut while I get a bandage."

Doria felt curiously honored by his confession. She was sure he wouldn't have made it to just anyone. As she watched him apply the bandage, a wealth of tenderness toward him welled up inside her that didn't have a thing to do with desire. That made it ultimately more threatening, because it bonded them on an emotional level. She couldn't let that happen.

She scurried back to the salad when he said, "All done."

"I knew it! It's your mother's spaghetti-sauce recipe!" Doria exclaimed in delight when she tasted it a short time later.

Matt smiled. "She always made it when you were coming for dinner. She said that she'd never seen anyone get so much enjoyment out of such a simple meal."

"It wasn't simple to me. I was the cook at my house, remember?"

"Boy, do I!" Matt laughed. "You were the only person I knew who could burn water."

"Well, you'll be pleased to know that my culinary skills have greatly improved. Some people consider me a gourmet chef," she bragged.

"If that's an invitation to dinner, I accept."

Doria sobered. "I don't think that would be a good idea."

"Because you're auditing my client?"

"That's part of it."

"And what's the rest?"

Unable to meet his penetrating gaze, Doria swirled her fork in the spaghetti. "There's been too much water under the bridge."

"You surprise me, Doria. I would never have guessed that you talk in clichés."

"Don't taunt me, Matt." She looked at him, her eyes wide and pleading. "I want to leave the past alone."

"Why?"

Doria rubbed at her temples, which were starting to pound. "It was a horrible place. A horrible time. I want—no, I need—to forget it."

"That's the coward's way out," he chided softly.

"So, I'm a coward."

"I don't believe that. You were one of the bravest people I've ever known."

"You're wrong, Matt. I was desperately afraid. I just put up a good front."

"And you don't have to put up a front now?"

"Of course I do, but it's different."

"How's it different?"

"What do you want from me?" she asked plaintively, not sure where the conversation was leading, but sensing that she wasn't going to like it.

"I don't know," he answered. "Maybe I want some reassurance that a part of the girl I knew still exists. Maybe I want you to convince me that what we shared as children wasn't part of your front—that we really were friends."

"Our friendship was not a front," she stated passionately. "That was real, Matt. I swear it."

"Then, how could you let me take the fall without even trying to help? And don't give me that crock about protecting my ego. I want to know the truth, Doria. I need to understand."

"Why?" she questioned belligerently. "Understanding won't change anything."

"It might stop me from hating you."

Doria had known he hated her, but for him to say so aloud was more than she could bear. She was out of her chair and flying toward the front door before she even realized what she was doing. When her hand curled around the doorknob, Matt grabbed her shoulders and spun her around.

"You're not going to keep running away from me!" he said harshly. "I want some answers, and by damn, you owe them to me. Why did you let me take the fall, Doria?"

Doria started to tell him to go to hell, but the words wouldn't come when she met his eyes. They were as tormented as she felt. She did owe him the truth, she realized. He'd still hate her, but at least he'd know why she'd betrayed him.

"If I'd been arrested again, I would have been sent to a foster home," she confessed miserably. "I know that sounds crazy. My father hated me, but he was all I had. I couldn't lose him."

"Oh, Doria," Matt murmured sympathetically as he hugged her close. When she wrapped her arms around his waist and buried her head against his chest, all the anger he'd harbored toward her died and was replaced with compassion. On its heels came a need to comfort and protect, which didn't surprise him; Doria had always brought out his protective instincts.

"I'm sorry, Matt," she whispered tearfully. "What I did to you was wrong, and I'll never forgive myself."

"You were just a kid," he soothed. "You were trying to survive in the only way you knew how. It's okay, Doria. I understand."

She leaned her head back and peered up at him. Matt's heart lurched at the tears rolling down her cheeks. In all the time he'd known her, he'd never seen her cry. The fact that he'd caused her such distress ripped him apart. He tracked the trail of tears with his fingertips.

Doria was mesmerized as Matt touched her cheek. The emotions flickering across his face were too swift to identify, but their message was clear. For the first time since they'd been reunited, she saw the warmth and caring she'd come to expect from him. She also saw raw physical need and responded to it on an elemental level.

When Matt began to lower his head, desire swelled through her. She wanted him to kiss her. She wanted him to make love to her, but she couldn't let it happen. She pressed her fingers to his lips. "No, Matt."

"Why not?" he muttered in frustration. "You want me as much as I want you. I can see it in your eyes."

"I do want you," Doria admitted, "but I'm auditing your client. I've worked too hard to build an impeccable reputation on the job. I won't risk it—not even for you."

"I'm not asking you to risk your reputation," Matt argued. "What's happening between us has nothing to do with Halliford."

"When two people are involved, they can't be objective," Doria rebutted. "We aren't the most even-tempered people in the first place. If we were lovers, we'd take everything that happens at the office personally, even if we swore we wouldn't. You know I'm right, Matt."

Matt wanted to disagree but couldn't. Their personalities were too volatile to mix business with pleasure. If he wanted to pursue her—and he definitely wanted to pursue her—then he had to wait.

"I'll back off for now, but when the audit is over, you're fair game," he told her.

A shiver that was a combination of expectancy and fear, raced through Doria. She eased out of his embrace. "I'd better go."

"You haven't finished dinner," Matt objected.

"Bring it to the office," Doria suggested as she opened the door and stepped onto the stoop. "Good night, Matt."

"Good night, Doria," he returned reluctantly.

Long after she was gone, he stood in the doorway and stared out into the night. He hadn't felt this mixed-up since he'd been sent to Denver. Irritated by his maudlin feelings, he fished for a cigarette, mumbling a curse when he came up empty. Tomorrow he'd buy a crate of cigarettes and write Uless a check. Staying away from Doria was going to be difficult enough. He didn't need the additional torture of nicotine cravings.

As if on cue, Uless and two members of the Sinners materialized in front of him. Matt scowled when Uless grinned and tossed him a bag of sunflower seeds. The sneaky punk had been in his desk and discovered his secret vice! Of all the low-down, dirty rotten tricks!

"I just found me a car," Uless announced with a pronounced snap of his gum, convincing Matt that he knew perfectly well that it drove his boss nuts. "All I need to buy it is another five hundred bucks."

"Well, I've always said that a man should have a dream," Matt drawled.

Uless laughed, then lowered his voice to a conspiratorial level. "Speaking of dreams, what happened between you and the lady treasury agent? I've never seen a woman hightail it so fast. You're starting to lose your touch, man. Maybe I should give you some pointers."

"Doria and I are just friends," Matt snapped impatiently.

"If that's true, then I'm really concerned. It means you've started wearing lipstick."

Matt brought his hand to his lips and realized that he'd been had, when Uless and his friends howled with laughter. "Cute, Uless."

"Ah, Matt, save your pretty words for the lady."

"I told you, we're just friends," he said with asperity.

"Well, keep the faith. I'm sure you'll find a way to overcome that problem. See you tomorrow."

"Not if I see you first," Matt grumbled, but he couldn't help smiling when the boys walked away.

He returned to the kitchen, but when he sat down at the table, he spent more time staring at his food than eating it. His thoughts were on Doria and everything she'd revealed tonight. Eventually, his mind homed in on the kiss they'd shared. Just the memory was enough to give him a hard-on that wouldn't quit.

"Well, hell," he groused as he tore open the bag of sunflower seeds and downed a handful. It was going to be a long night.

NORMALLY, DORIA FOUND her apartment soothing. Tonight, however, it felt alien. She studied the living room, wondering what it would look like to a stranger or, more specifically, to Matt.

She didn't have a lot of furniture, but what pieces she did have were expensive and built to last. Her decorating scheme was earth tones and pastels. Everything was orderly and clean, but it suddenly struck her that there were no individual touches to add personality to the room.

Most people had family photographs and plants and personal treasures displayed. She had no family photographs. And she had a black thumb when it came to any type of gardening. The only personal treasure she had was a pendant that had belonged to her mother and turned her skin green if she wore it.

"You're more alone today then you were fourteen years ago," Matt had said. The truth of those words had never been more evident.

"Damn him," she muttered as she headed for her bedroom, refusing to be depressed. She'd been completely satisfied with her life before Matt had come along, and she'd be satisfied with it when he was gone.

Even as she came to that conclusion, Doria knew it wouldn't be that simple. Tonight Matt had kissed her and opened a floodgate of feelings that weren't going to go away easily. He'd also said that once the audit was over, she'd be fair game. He hadn't meant it as a threat, but she perceived it as one.

She sat on the edge of her bed and wrapped her arms around her middle. She was attracted to Matt, but was she responding to the man he was today or the boy she'd adored so many years ago? And what about him? Was he responding to her, the woman, or to the girl she used to be?

They were complicated questions made even more complex by her betrayal of him. Tonight he'd seemed willing to forgive her, but he'd hated her for fourteen years. Could he really dismiss those feelings in a matter of hours?

With an abject groan, Doria fell back on her bed, feeling more confused than she had when she'd left Matt's house.

The audit had bought her some time, but eventually it would be over. When it was, she was going to have to be ready to deal with Matt.

# 5

"HEY, CHILL OUT," Uless griped as Matt paced in front of his desk. "You're not only making me dizzy, you're wearing out the carpet."

"To hell with the carpet," Matt muttered. "Doria should have been here an hour ago."

"I'm sure she's stuck in traffic. The freeways are murder during rush hour."

Matt knew that Uless was only trying to reassure him, but his bad choice of words evoked the image of Doria's small car. Her job required her to spend a great deal of time on the road. She should be driving a tank, not a piece of tinfoil!

"Are you sure she got home last night?" Uless asked. "She did have to drive through some mean streets to get to the freeway."

The image Matt invoked this time brought him to a halt. His neighborhood was fairly crime-free, even without the Sinners help. Some of the surrounding neighborhoods, however, weren't safe in daylight. He knew to avoid them, but Doria would have taken the most direct route. Why hadn't he escorted her to the freeway? What if she hadn't locked her doors? What if her car had broken down? What if—

"Where in hell have you been?" he demanded in a deadly rasp when Doria chose that moment to walk through the door. He'd been worried sick about her, and she had the audacity to stand there with every hair in place!

Doria was shocked by Matt's tone. She took a cautious step back as she regarded him. She'd never seen him so furious, and she hoped she never did again.

A shiver of uneasiness traced her spine. "I had to stop by my office."

"Why didn't you call?"

Her temper stirred. "I don't work for you, Matt. I don't have to check in."

Instead of responding, he hooked his thumbs in his belt loops and advanced on her with a loose-limbed gait that was decidedly predatory. Oddly enough, it wasn't fear churning in her stomach. It was that hot and reckless feeling that he seemed to incite in her. When he reached her, she gazed up at him in belligerent challenge.

"You may not work for me, Doria, but you *will* check in if you're going to be late," he stated emphatically.

Doria knew she was pushing, but she couldn't seem to stop herself from taunting him. "And if I don't? What are you going to do? Beat me up?"

If he'd been furious before, it was nothing compared to the rage that leaped into his eyes now. "No, Doria. I'll do something much worse than that."

Doria told herself not to take the bait, but again she couldn't seem to stop herself. "And what would be worse than that?"

"I'll call your boss and insist that you be taken off this audit because of our past."

"You wouldn't dare," she challenged, though the involuntary quaver in her voice belied her bravado.

"Suit yourself." He turned and walked toward his office, saying cheerfully, "Uless, would you get Mrs. Anderson's file and bring it to me? I need to call her about her estimated taxes."

"Sure thing," Uless replied.

Doria was still standing where Matt had left her when he closed the door behind him. She was seething, and she couldn't decide if she wanted to scream or stomp her feet. How *dare* he use the threat of her job to get her to do what he wanted!

"He's mad because he was worried about you," Uless stated with a look of commiseration.

"He has no right to be worried about me," Doria declared, becoming angrier. *Damn the man's propensity for making every dispute between them a spectacle!*

"Well, he was worried, anyway. It goes with the territory, if you know what I mean."

"Matt and I are just friends," Doria informed him.

"Which is exactly my point." Uless spun his chair around, pulled a file out of the file cabinet and rose to his feet. He winked at her. "I worry about my friends, too. Considering Matt's mood, I'd better get this in to him. See you later."

Doria cursed softly when Uless strolled into Matt's office. He'd been talking about friendship, and she'd intimated that there was more going on. When was she going to learn to keep her mouth shut?

She marched to her office, not even bothering to grab a cup of coffee. She didn't need caffeine. Her clash with Matt had provided her with enough adrenaline to complete a day's work in an hour. If he made her this angry every morning, she'd be able to complete this audit in a week!

Visions of revenge stirred in her mind, but when she found herself being more critical with the Halliford account than necessary, she reeled her temper back in. She wasn't going to take her anger out on his client. She'd reserve every ounce of it for Matt.

MATT STARED OUT the window despondently. He'd told Uless to hold his calls and not disturb him for any reason. He knew he was sulking, but he felt like sulking.

Two days had passed since he'd given Doria that damnable ultimatum, and outside of discussions regarding Halliford, she wouldn't speak to him. He didn't blame her. He should have never threatened her, but when she'd insinuated that he'd actually strike her, something inside him had snapped. If she'd give him the opportunity, he'd apologize in a flash. Unfortunately, it appeared that she had no intention of letting him apologize. And it was driving him crazy.

His bout of self-pity was interrupted by a burst of uproarious laughter. He ignored it, but when it grew louder and part of it was distinctly feminine, his curiosity was aroused. He walked to the door and pulled it open.

The scene that met his eyes didn't improve his bad mood. Uless and Doria were being entertained by Raul Delgado. Raul was one of the best defense attorneys in Los Angeles and had been on the city's list of most eligible bachelors for three years running. He was staring at Doria with blatant interest, and the bright smile Doria was giving him made Matt curl his hand around the doorknob in a death grip.

Raul was exactly the type of man who would appeal to Doria's Yuppie tastes. He may have grown up on the streets, but he was handsome, polished charm from the top of his expensively styled, glistening black hair to the tips of his gleaming Italian loafers. Even his underwear probably sported designer labels!

"I didn't know we had an appointment, Raul," he said, forcing himself to be polite when what he wanted to do was beat his friend to a pulp.

"We didn't," Raul replied, not bothering to glance in Matt's direction. It was obvious that he only had eyes for Doria. "I was in the area and thought we might have lunch.

Uless says you're busy, so Doria has agreed to keep me company."

*Over my dead body!* Matt fumed. Aloud, he said, "Doria works for the government, Raul. She only gets an hour for lunch." Even to Matt, his words sounded ridiculous, but it was all he'd been able to think of on such short notice.

"That's okay. I'll have her back in an hour."

Before Matt could come up with another argument, Raul escorted Doria out the door.

"Damn!" he exploded.

Uless snapped his gum and threw a book at him. Matt automatically caught it and then scowled down at the sexy cover. "What in hell is this?"

"A romance novel," Uless answered. "Read it. You might learn something."

"I don't need a book to tell me how to romance a woman," Matt snapped.

Uless grinned. "If that's true, then why is the lady treasury agent having lunch with Don Juan?"

"Wiseass," Matt retorted as he slammed the door and stalked back to his chair. It was only when he was seated that he realized he still had the book.

He started to toss it aside, but had an hour to kill before Doria returned from lunch. He tore open a new bag of sunflower seeds and turned to the teaser page. He arched a brow as he read it. Maybe he'd been underestimating the romance genre. This sounded like some pretty hot stuff.

"WHERE HAVE YOU BEEN all my life?" Raul asked Doria. They were seated in a small Mexican restaurant that was little more than a dive. Raul had assured her, however, that it served the best Mexican food in town.

"I'm a lowly treasury agent," Doria said with a laugh. "I don't travel in your illustrious circles."

"Ah, yes, another blackball against fame and fortune," he mourned melodramatically. The waitress arrived, and while he ordered for them in rapid Spanish, Doria studied him.

She hadn't met Raul until today, but she knew everything about him—or at least as much as she'd read in the newspapers. His family had immigrated from Mexico when he was a baby. His parents had been migrant farm workers until his father lost a leg in a farming accident. They'd ended up in one of Los Angeles's worst barrios.

Despite the odds, Raul had landed a full scholarship to Harvard, where he'd gone on to Harvard law school. He'd returned to Los Angeles as a public defender. After winning a couple of highly publicized cases, he'd been offered a job at a top law firm in Beverly Hills. Today, he was one of the most sought-after defense attorneys among the rich and famous, but it was his *pro bono* cases that gave him notoriety. He was a champion of the underdog, which made him a media darling. Of course, his infamous love life added plenty of spice to that image, though Doria wondered if the reports were true. Raul was an incorrigible flirt, but she suspected it was an act. There was something about him she identified with. She had a feeling that it was because they were both living lies.

"I think I'm in love with you, Doria," he said with an engaging grin when the waitress walked away. "Let's pack our bags and run off to Tahiti. We'll bask in the sun, drink pineapple juice and make babies."

Doria laughed again. "As nice as that sounds, I'm afraid I have to decline. I sunburn easily, I hate pineapple juice, and I'm not ready for motherhood."

"You've just broken my heart," he lamented.

"You'll feel better as soon as you've eaten," Doria assured.

"You're right of course. Nothing's better for a broken heart than a superb enchilada. So, tell me, what's going on between you and Matt?"

Doria, caught off guard by the unexpected question, said, "Why would you ask me something like that?"

He chuckled. "Come on, Doria. Matt was practically foaming at the mouth when he found out we were going to lunch."

"Don't be ridiculous."

"Believe me, I'm not. I'm also damn curious. Matt isn't normally the jealous type."

"There's nothing going on between us," Doria stated firmly. "I'm auditing his client, and that's it. End of story."

"Whatever you say," Raul murmured agreeably, but the searching look he gave her made her squirm in her chair.

Thankfully, their food arrived, which occupied his attention. Doria knew that he hadn't reached the pinnacle of success by accident. Part of a good defense attorney's stock-in-trade was his ability to spot a lie. If Raul figured out that there was more than business going on between her and Matt, he might feel obligated to report it. How had she managed to get herself into such a mess?

*By betraying a friend fourteen years ago,* her conscience was quick to answer. Doria accepted that simple truth. If she hadn't betrayed Matt, they'd still be friends, which meant she wouldn't be auditing Halliford.

That old saying "What goes around, comes around" flashed through her mind. She had a terrible feeling that she would soon get what was coming to her.

MATT WAS ABSORBED in the romance novel. As far as he was concerned, the Yuppie hero, Drake, was a bit of a wimp. Nevertheless, he sure knew how to handle the prickly heroine, who was so reminiscent of Doria, it was eerie. Drake was also doing a great job of seducing her without even touching her, which Matt found fascinating.

Was it possible that a little flirting and some well-timed chest baring might crumble Doria's walls? It seemed a bit heavy-handed, but it might be worth considering. After all, Doria was at lunch with smooth-talking Raul. He was probably sweeping her off her feet by plying her with imported sparkling spring water and tofu!

When Uless cracked open the door to announce he was leaving for school, Matt gave an absent wave in acknowledgement. Then he plopped the bag of sunflower seeds into his lap, propped his feet on the desk and leaned back in his chair. The book was getting hot and heavy, both in plot and seduction. He couldn't put it down.

When the phone rang, he was into a particularly steamy scene and ignored it. When it stopped ringing, he felt a twinge of guilt. He soothed it by reaching for another handful of sunflower seeds and promising himself that as soon as he finished this scene, he'd quit reading—not only for business reasons, but because he was getting turned-on.

He'd just flipped the page when his door opened. Startled by the unexpected interruption, he vaulted to his feet. The sunflower-seed bag went flying in one direction and the book in the other. Doria was standing in the doorway looking at him in wide-eyed surprise, and he felt his cheeks flush with embarrassment. If she got a good look at the book cover, he'd never live it down.

"Dammit, Doria, didn't you ever learn to knock?" he yelled.

"Well, excuse me," Doria said indignantly as she stalked into his office and slapped a phone message onto his desk. "When you didn't answer your phone, I assumed you were out and took a message. Believe me, I won't be so rude as to do something nice for you again." With that, she stalked back out, slamming the door behind her.

Matt ground his teeth in frustration. Doria had been mad before, but now she was livid. When was he going to learn to control his temper?

He stomped over to the romance novel, scooped it up and scowled at the cover. He could almost see good old Drake shaking his head in disgust over Matt's actions. Drake's heroine was even more temperamental than Doria, but he never yelled at her. He just turned on the charm and shed his silk shirt. He'd probably learned everything he knew from Raul.

Well, he wasn't Drake or Raul. He was Matt Cutter, and he was tired of playing games with Doria. He hurled the book toward his desk and headed after her. If she wanted to be mad at him, she could kick and scream and throw things like a normal person. The silent treatment was going to stop!

Doria wasn't surprised when Matt stormed into her office, his expression clearly stating that he was spoiling for a fight. What did surprise her was that she was also spoiling for one. Normally, she avoided confrontations. Shouting matches were not civilized. Then again, in order to behave like a civilized person, you had to be dealing with one. Matt reached her desk and slammed his hands down on top of it, acting like he was a throwback to the Neanderthal period.

He leaned toward her, snarling, "All right, Doria. I've had it. Just what in hell do you think you're doing?"

Doria bit her inner cheek and tapped her pencil against the file in front of her. She was *not* going to snarl back. "I'm doing my job—or at least I would be if I didn't have to answer your phone and put up with your rude interruptions."

"Stop using that haughty tone with me!" he ordered so thunderously that Doria would have sworn the windows rattled.

"Haughty tone?" she repeated disparagingly. "For your information, I am speaking calmly and rationally. Unlike you, I don't have to bellow to get my point across."

His eyes narrowed to slits. "No, you just clam up. Well, I'm not going to put up with it any longer. Either you start talking to me, or—"

"Or what?" Doria interrupted, incensed. "You'll call my boss? Let's do it now!" She made a grab for the receiver, but Matt was faster. His fingers curled around her wrist.

"I don't need to call your boss to straighten this out," he rasped. "As Drake would say, there are far easier ways to deal with a woman like you."

Doria gazed at him in bewilderment. Who was Drake, and just how *did* he deal with a woman like her? One look into Matt's eyes gave her the answer. They were filled with lust.

"Let me go, Matt," she whispered hoarsely, while desperately fighting against the hot, responding wave of desire rolling through her. How could she be so angry with him and want him so badly at the same time?

"All in good time," Matt replied as he angled his way around her desk.

"You're hurting me," she accused as she tried unsuccessfully to jerk her hand out of his. It was a lie, but it was the only way she could think of to escape him, and she needed to escape him. The heat in her middle was growing hotter by the second.

"That's not true, Doria. You know I'd never hurt you."

By this time, he was standing in front of her, and she rolled her chair back until she rammed into the wall. Matt followed, never once easing his grip on her wrist. When he had her trapped, he did release it and dropped a hand on either arm of her chair. Then he leaned toward her. Doria knew he was going to kiss her, but she was powerless to stop him.

"Matt, please—" She shook her head frantically as his lips came closer, but her words were more a request than a denial.

"Of course, I'll please you," he murmured as his mouth came down over hers and his tongue plunged inside.

The first kiss they'd shared had been ravishing, but it was nothing compared to the hard, hungry one he treated her to this time. Stars were flickering against the backs of her eyelids. Sparks were shooting off inside her. Her breasts grew taut. She became hot and moist between her thighs. She'd never been so instantly aroused, yet the only parts of their bodies touching were their lips.

When Matt suddenly broke away from the kiss, Doria was so stunned that she couldn't open her eyes. She dropped her head back against her chair and gasped for breath.

"Look at me," Matt commanded, his voice rough and gritty. It was a long moment before Doria could comply, but when she did, he said, "That's what is waiting for us when this audit is over. I told you I'd keep my distance until then, and I'm trying my damnedest to do so. If you keep playing games with me, however, all bets are off. So stay the hell away from Raul. Got that?"

Doria knew she should tell him she'd see Raul if she wanted to, but she nodded, because she couldn't have spoken if she'd had to.

"Good girl," he pronounced, and then treated her to a surprisingly tender smile. "You look beautiful with your lipstick smeared. I can't wait to muss up the rest of you."

With that he walked out, and Doria raised a trembling hand to her lips. As impossible as it seemed, in that one brief, blazing kiss, Matt had laid claim to her heart—or perhaps it was better to say he'd reclaimed it. What was she going to do?

DORIA COULDN'T concentrate. She laid her pencil on the file she'd been working on and went to the window. Matt was the cause of her agitation. It had been ten days since he'd given her that heart-stealing kiss. Since then, he'd been such a perfect gentleman that she was beginning to wonder if he was sick.

Matt wasn't the polite, cordial type. He was a man who knew what he wanted and went after it. When he'd kissed her so passionately, she'd thought he wanted her. Now she was beginning to think she'd imagined the entire incident.

Her thoughts were interrupted by a light rap on her open door. She smiled when she saw Uless. Her initial wariness of him had been replaced by cautious fondness. He was bright, amusing and hardworking. She still hadn't resolved that he was the leader of the Sinners, so she ignored that part of his life.

"What can I do for you, Uless?"

"Here are the bills of lading and invoices you wanted from Halliford," he answered as he strolled into her office and placed the files on her desk.

"Thanks," Doria told him as she returned to her chair. When he didn't leave immediately, she asked, "Was there something else?"

He ducked his head in an uncharacteristically shy gesture, "Could I ask you a personal question?"

Doria's guard went up. "I suppose that depends on how personal it is."

"It's not *personal* personal. I just need some advice about my girlfriend."

"Okay," Doria said carefully. She hoped this wasn't going to be one of those heavy-duty, man-woman questions. She was the last person in the world to be giving advice on relationships.

Uless dropped into the chair next to her desk. "Her birthday's coming up and I want to give her something special. You know, something that no one else would give her. But I don't have a lot of money. I thought you might be able to suggest a unique gift."

"I can try. Why don't you tell me about her?" She was charmed by the adoring smile that curved his lips.

"Sally's the kindest, sweetest person I've ever met, but she's had a tough couple of years. Her father died and she goes to school and works to help support her younger brother and sister. Then, of course, there was the mugging. Thank God, Matt was there and saved her."

Doria immediately perked up. "Matt saved Sally from a mugging?"

"Yeah. You didn't know?"

Doria shook her head. "What happened?"

Uless's expression turned so hard that Doria shivered. This was exactly how she'd envisioned the leader of the Sinners—cold and lethal.

"Sally was coming home from work when some junkie tried to mug her. When he found out she didn't have any money, he decided to slice her up."

Bile rose in Doria's throat as she pictured the scene he'd just described. "And Matt saved her?"

"Yeah. He was out doing one of his good-deed tours, and he saw the guy drag her into the alley. He went in after them."

"Then Sally was all right?"

"She had a black eye and some bruises, but Matt wasn't so lucky. He had to have forty-eight stitches in his arm and nearly that many on his chest." Uless gave a disbelieving shake of his head. "I was convinced he was crazy. I mean, what man in his right mind would take on a drugged-out freak with a knife when he was unarmed? Of course, now that I know Matt, I understand. He is crazy, but it's a good kind of crazy. Know what I mean?"

"Yes," Doria answered, recalling some of Matt's good-guy-to-the-rescue escapades during his younger years. Like Uless, she'd thought he was crazy, but she hadn't been able to fault him. How could you criticize courage, even if it was a stupid move? "How did you end up working for Matt?"

"He conned me," Uless replied with a dry chuckle. "When I asked him what I could do to pay him back for saving Sally, he told me I had to go back to school and get my high-school diploma. Then he offered me this job to help make ends meet."

"And you accepted because you felt you owed him."

"It's the code. He saved Sally's life," Uless said with a shrug. "Let's get back to this birthday present. Do you have any ideas?"

"What kind of apartment does she live in?"

"Better than some, but worse than most."

"Why don't you paint her apartment?" Doria suggested, remembering the gloomy, paint-chipped walls of the apartment she'd grown up in. Coming home had been like walking into a dungeon. It was hard to dream of a better life when you were faced with squalor.

"That's a great idea!" Uless said with enthusiasm. "Paint wouldn't cost that much, and I might even have enough left over so she could buy material to make new curtains."

Doria got caught up in his excitement. "Better yet, talk Matt into letting you do some work on his house in exchange for the paint. Then she'd not only be able to make new curtains, you'd have enough left over to take her to dinner."

Uless laughed. "I like the way your mind thinks. Thanks."

"You're welcome," Doria answered, feeling inordinately pleased with herself.

It was only after Uless was gone that she recalled him saying that Matt had stumbled upon Sally's mugging while out doing one of his good-deed tours. Just what kind of good deeds was Matt doing? She considered following Uless and asking, but did she really want to know?

*Forty-eight stitches in his arm and nearly that many on his chest.*

Doria felt sick at the realization that it could just as easily have been a deadly stab to the heart. For a man who got queasy at the sight of blood, Matt certainly was hanging out in the wrong neighborhoods.

But he had always been a paradox. Tough and gentle. Fierce and kind. Bad and good. He'd risk his life for a stranger, and Doria could only imagine to what lengths he'd go to protect the woman he loved.

A part of her wondered what it would be like to be that woman, but she dismissed the fanciful thought. Her life-style didn't allow for a man like Matt. Indeed, her life-style didn't allow for *any* man; and that was the saddest fact of all.

With a weary sigh, she reached for the files she'd requested from Halliford. Outside of a few minor discrepancies, Halliford's records were impeccable, and that was the problem. They were *too* impeccable. It didn't mean that they were doing anything wrong, but if they were, she was convinced that this was where she'd find it.

MATT WOULD HAVE SWORN that passing his CPA exam had been the hardest challenge of his life, but it was proving to be a piece of cake compared to keeping his hands off Doria for the past two weeks.

It was Raul's and Uless's fault, he thought grumpily as he dressed for work. If Raul hadn't taken Doria to lunch, Uless wouldn't have given him that damn romance novel. If he hadn't been reading it when she'd walked into his office, he wouldn't have been embarrassed and yelled at her. If he hadn't yelled at her, she wouldn't have stalked off. If she hadn't stalked off, he wouldn't have followed and given her that fiery kiss that had left him in perpetual arousal ever since. Then again, if he hadn't threatened to call her boss if she didn't check in, none of the other events would have happened. That meant he was the one at fault. He hated it when his conscience made him take responsibility for his own actions.

He sighed in resignation as he grabbed a book from the large stack beside his bed, wrapped it in a small brown paper bag, and tucked it into his jacket pocket with his sunflower seeds. He'd read that when a person quit smoking, they developed another vice to replace it. To his annoyance, he was hooked on sunflower seeds and romance novels. It was enough to make a man question his sanity.

On his way to the office, he decided that he could kick the sunflower-seed habit by simply lighting up. The romance novels wouldn't be that easy. The only cure for them would be a good tussle between the sheets with Doria.

Just the thought made him break out in a sweat. He'd made love to Doria so many times in his dreams that he was sure he'd come up with a half-dozen new positions. The trouble was, the moment they reached the point of climax, he woke up.

It wasn't the first time he'd been faced with sexual frustration, and he doubted it would be the last. Even during his youth he hadn't been able to hop into bed with every

Mary, Jane and Sue that came along. Physical attraction wasn't enough for him. He had to connect with a woman on an emotional level.

He was connecting emotionally with Doria, though he didn't understand why. She was so proper. So controlled. He'd also lost count of the number of designer-label suits she owned. Just once, he'd like to see her dressed in a pair of worn denims and her hair standing on end. Then he'd feel as if she were human.

When he pulled up in front of his office, Doria was getting out of her car. When she walked toward him a minute later, he decided that if he could package that sexy little sway of her hips, he'd be a millionaire overnight.

"Good morning," he said gruffly when she reached him. "What's new?"

"Good morning," Doria replied. She forced herself to keep her eyes on his face and not his thighs, which gripped the bike in a particularly provocative manner. "And besides the day, my shoes are new. Do you own a car, or are you strictly a motorcycle kind of guy?"

"I own a car, but the bike's cheaper to operate. It's also less polluting," he answered as he eyed her shoes. They were serviceable, tan leather pumps. There was nothing alluring about them, yet Matt found them to be a turn-on. Perhaps it was because they emphasized the narrow daintiness of her feet. He dragged his eyes back to her face when his mind started making erotic suggestions of what he could do to her toes. "The bike's my contribution to cleaning up the air."

"What kind of car is it?" Doria asked in a voice that sounded oddly breathless. It didn't surprise her. She seemed to have trouble breathing whenever she was around Matt. "A sporty red racer?"

Matt chuckled as he climbed to his feet. "No. It's a minivan about the same color as your shoes."

Doria's eyes widened in surprise. "Why do you own something that big?"

"How else am I going to seduce young maidens in comfort?" he teased as he took her arm and led her toward the door.

Doria knew he was joking, but that didn't stop the flare of jealousy that shot through her. Good heavens, she was in worse shape than she'd thought! Jealousy had never been a part of her makeup. She'd always felt that if you had to be that concerned about a man, then he wasn't worth the trouble.

Of course, the man had to be a part of your life before you could be concerned about him. Outside of work, Matt didn't exist. Unless you counted dreams. He'd definitely been hanging around in that arena. She turned her mind to business before it could recall some of those fantasies. They were too hot to handle asleep. She had no intention of reliving them awake.

"I've found some discrepancies between Halliford's invoices and their shipping documents," she told him as they approached his office.

"What kind of discrepancies?" Matt asked, immediately switching into a working mode. He wasn't involved in Halliford's day-to-day operations that involved shipping-and-billing documentation. All he received was a monthly accounting of their activities. Since their figures had never seemed out of line, he'd never had reason to question them.

"It's the descriptions of merchandise," Doria answered. "There's probably nothing wrong, but I'd like to inspect the goods at the warehouse as soon as possible. Can you arrange it for me?"

"Sure." He opened the door for her. "I'll see if we can go over there this afternoon."

"You don't have to go with me, Matt. I can handle this on my own."

He gave her one of his determined looks. "I'm going with you, Doria. Halliford's my client. If there's a problem, I want to be there when it's found."

Doria started to object, but changed her mind. As Matt said, Halliford was his client, and it wasn't unusual for an accountant to accompany her on an inspection. She wasn't sure why she didn't want Matt along.

Well, that wasn't true. Just the sight of him had a volatile effect on her senses, and it hurt that she didn't seem to have the same effect on him. Yes, she definitely had it bad, which was ridiculous. She should be showering heaven with prayers of thanks for his disinterest.

"I'll let you know what I find out," Matt told her as he walked into his office.

Doria didn't answer. She was too busy watching his backside, and she concluded that it should be unlawful for a man to have such cute buns. She'd barely had time to settle at her desk when Matt popped into her office.

"Halliford wants to know if you can hold off until tomorrow afternoon. Most of their warehouse personnel will be in a safety-training session, so the place will be deserted. It seems that their insurance company frowns on visitors in the warehouse during working hours, even if they are from the IRS."

"Tomorrow's fine," Doria answered. "Did you tell them what the problem was?"

Matt shook his head and dropped into the chair beside her desk. "If they're doing something wrong, I want to know about it. Nothing can ruin a CPA's reputation faster than association with a crooked company."

"I don't think they're doing anything crooked," Doria assured as she retrieved two documents from the files in question. "As I said, it's descriptions of merchandise. For instance, the bill of lading for this account says that they shipped two hundred body stockings, but the invoice bills the company for two hundred cat suits, which I assume is a costume. The stock numbers match, so shipping is probably using the descriptions printed on the boxes, while accounting is using the descriptions that marketing developed to sell the product."

Matt nodded thoughtfully. "I can see where you'd question them. You need to make sure that they're costing the proper goods. How many discrepancies have you found?"

"I have one month's records, and at least half of them disagree."

Matt let out a low whistle. "May I see the files?"

Doria started to hand them to him, but when he extended his arm, her gaze was caught by a thin, pink scar that ran from the inside of his elbow down to his wrist. Uless's words skipped through her mind. "Matt wasn't so lucky. Forty-eight stitches in his arm and nearly that many on his chest."

"Doria, is something wrong?" Matt asked when the color drained from her face.

"That scar on your arm. Is it from when you saved Uless's girlfriend?"

Matt's eyes widened in surprise. "Who told you about that?"

"Uless. How could you risk your life like that?"

"It sounds as if Uless has been exaggerating," Matt mumbled as he pulled his arm back and tucked it against his side, feeling self-conscious.

"Don't try to mollify me," Doria said, unable to keep her eyes from wandering over the breadth of his chest. The thought of a scar marring it caused a wrenching ache inside. "I've seen you in action, Matt. You have the heart of a hero and the brains of a fool."

"Thanks a lot," he grumbled. "You really know how to boost a man's ego."

Doria searched his face. "Why do you keep going back? You've become something. Why can't you let go of the past?"

"Because it's my roots. I may have made it out, but I can't turn my back on the problems."

"You think you can solve them when an entire nation can't?" Doria questioned heatedly. "As I said, you have the brains of a fool."

"That's probably what people said about the founders of our country, but they were a handful of people who made a difference."

"And you think that you alone can make a difference?" she scoffed.

"I'm not alone. I belong to a group of professional men and women who grew up on the streets and beat the odds. They're people like me and Raul Delgado, and we aren't gullible enough to believe that we can solve the entire mess. What we do believe is that one success is worth our time and energy. We also hope that every person we save will save another. If we can get a chain reaction going, we may be able to wipe out the ghetto environment entirely."

"It won't happen in your lifetime," Doria noted dryly.

"It probably won't," Matt agreed. "But the problem didn't occur in one lifetime, either. Why don't you join us, Doria? You're a fabulous success story, and we need more women who have made it."

"Absolutely not!" Doria responded with a vehement shake of her head.

"Why not?" Matt asked in confusion. "If it's time you're worried about, that's no problem. Most of the group can only spare a couple of days a month."

"I don't care if it's only a couple of days a year. I'm not interested."

"You're afraid," he surmised.

She glared at him. "Of course, I'm afraid. Look what happened to you."

"That was an isolated incident. I happened to be in the wrong place at the right time. You wouldn't be going in alone. You'd be part of a group."

"I'm not interested," Doria insisted. "Do you want to look at these files?"

Matt accepted the files she thrust at him while eyeing her thoughtfully. "How long are you going to run from your past, Doria?"

"I am not running," she stated in slow, measured tones that stressed her rising temper. "I'm being realistic. I'm not a trained social worker or a therapist. I have nothing to offer those people."

"You're wrong. You can offer yourself as an example."

"I don't *want* to be an example!" she exclaimed stridently.

"Why?" Matt demanded, leaning toward her. "What are you afraid of? And don't tell me that it's a fear of being hurt. It's more than that."

"You're right. It is more than that. I've built a new life for myself. No one knows about my past, and I don't want them to know about it. I don't want to face their stares. I don't want to answer their questions. Most of all, I don't want their pity."

"I don't think people will pity you as much as they'll admire you," Matt countered.

Doria shook her head again. "You're not listening to me, Matt. I don't want their admiration. I just want to fit in."

"And hiding your past helps you fit in? You can't believe that. What's more, if you really want to fit in, then you have to face your past. It's the only way you can be free."

"And doing volunteer work in the ghetto is going to accomplish this miracle?" Doria said derisively. "I'm not stupid, Matt. I also know that you and your friends are nothing more than a bunch of dabbling do-gooders who do more harm than good. You strut around the streets saying, 'Hey, look at me! I'm hot stuff.' You aren't trying to help. You're stroking your egos."

Matt was both hurt and infuriated by her words, but he again relied on patience instead of anger. "You're wrong, Doria."

"Am I?" she demanded harshly. "Can you honestly tell me that you don't come home feeling full of yourself after telling all those kids what a *success* you've become? I've been there, Matt. I've watched people like you come in with your good intentions, only to realize that what you really want is for me to drop at your feet and accord you the reverence that you think you deserve."

She gave an impatient wave of her hand as she continued. "I'm supposed to look at you and say, 'This man is right. I can be more than I am.' Then I go back to my rat-infested hovel and a moldy loaf of bread that I dug out of someone's garbage. I see my fifteen-year-old sister shoot up heroin or snort a line of coke to help her forget that she's heading for the street corner in hopes of earning a few dollars on her back to buy milk for her illegitimate baby. I watch my ten-year-old brother arm himself with enough weapons to qualify himself as a Third World nation before he leaves to meet his friends. I hear my mother cry because she was mugged or raped on the way to the corner grocery, and then I listen to my father beat the hell out of her for giving her assailant the money instead of coming home with a six-pack of beer.

"But you're right," she concluded scornfully. "I know I can make it out of the ghetto, because people like you tell me I can."

"My God, Doria, why are you so bitter?" Matt asked, shocked by her diatribe.

Doria leaned back in her chair and rubbed the bridge of her nose with her thumb and forefinger. "I'm not bitter. I'm sensible. I fought my way out of the ghetto and I'm not going back."

Matt wanted to push the issue, because he sensed that there was more. He realized, however, that this was neither the time nor the place to talk about it.

"I'll look at these files in my office," he told her as he rose to his feet. "Take it easy, okay?"

Doria glanced up at him and then quickly away when she saw the concern in his eyes. She didn't want his concern. She just wanted to go back to her nice, uncomplicated life that didn't have anything to do with the past.

When Matt was gone, she had to admit that part of what he'd said was true. She was running. From her past. From her father. Even from Matt. But most of all, she was running from herself.

# 6

"DAMN, MATT! What are you trying to do out there? Kill me?" Raul complained as they stumbled off the cracked basketball court.

For the past hour they'd been in a no-holds-barred game with a group of kids they'd been working with for two years. One of the boys had recently won a basketball scholarship to UCLA. Matt couldn't have been more proud if the young man had been his own son.

He grabbed a towel and mopped his face. "You know what they say, Raul. If you can't stand the heat, then stay out of the fire."

Raul muttered a colorful Spanish curse as he grabbed a towel. "I said a long time ago that you were loco. Now I have proof that I'm right. Your bony elbows have bruised me from head to toe."

"I guess that means you'll be hiding from the paparazzi for a few weeks. Or maybe you can tell them that one of your gorgeous lovers just can't control herself when she's around you."

Raul responded with a derisive snort. "Don't believe everything you read, Matt. My press is far better than my love life."

"That's what you always say, but then I open the paper and see you dressed in a penguin suit with Miss Bosom of the Year hanging on your arm."

"Someone has to be her escort," Raul quipped.

"Of course, and you, being the gentleman that you are, feel obligated to put yourself at her disposal. How many women do you have on the string now? Twenty? Thirty?"

Raul chuckled. "You're just picking on me because I took Doria to lunch."

"I am not," Matt denied with a scowl. "Doria's a treasury agent auditing my client. If she wants to go to lunch with you, that's her prerogative."

"Sure, and tomorrow I'm going to be elected president," Raul muttered. "I'm not stupid, Matt. The sparks flying between you two are palpable. Put me out of my misery and tell me what's going on."

"You mean you couldn't con Doria into confiding the sordid story?" Matt drawled with mild sarcasm. "You'd better be careful, Raul. If those fancy partners of yours learn that you can't get a simple confession out of a treasury agent, you could end up in a ratty office next to mine."

"I've ended up in worse places." Raul sat down on the cement and patted the spot beside him. "Sit down and tell me your troubles."

Matt was too restless to sit. Instead, he wrapped the towel around his neck and gripped the ends as he watched the boys race around the court. "Why are we down here?" he asked. "Is it an ego trip?"

"I suppose that's possible," Raul answered. "Does it matter?"

"Yes," Matt stated forcefully. "I don't want to be here because of my ego. I want to be here because what I'm doing is important."

"What you're doing *is* important. If it's ego bringing you here, so be it. At least you're involved, and that's more than can be said for most people."

"Why do you do it?" Matt asked next.

Raul shrugged. "I went from a boy who had nothing to a man who has everything. I need this to ground me. It's my ticket to reality."

"Do you have any regrets about how your life's turned out?"

"Sure," Raul answered matter-of-factly. "I live like a king, but I've never been more lonely. Believe me, Matt, you don't know what ego is until you've been around some of the women I've dated. Their idea of slumming is going to a mall. I'd give anything to find a woman with some substance to her. You know the type. A rebel with a cause. Unfortunately, I've become so dissolute that I'd probably blow it. I'm not very good at dealing with rebels."

"You're underestimating yourself, Raul. Look how well you deal with these kids."

"That's because they don't demand anything of consequence from me. As far as they're concerned, I'm just another body to beat up on the basketball court. But you live in their world and speak their language. When you say something, they listen, because they know you care."

"They may listen to me, but they cheer you when you save one of them from going to prison for a crime they didn't commit."

"I have my moments," Raul agreed with a wry smile. "But they're few and far between, compared to yours. I'd give anything to be like you. You're a bridge between both worlds. You're as at home on this basketball court as you'd be at the Academy Awards ceremony with Miss Bosom of the Year on your arm."

"I wouldn't be caught dead at the Academy Awards ceremony," Matt proclaimed disdainfully. "I'd have to wear a tux."

Raul burst into hearty laughter as he climbed to his feet. He clapped Matt on the back. "You've got me there, my man. Shall we rejoin the game? I don't know about you, but I need some more ego bruising."

"You go ahead. I'm still catching my breath."

Raul nodded and jogged back onto the court. Matt watched the game with absentminded interest while his mind mulled over their conversation. It was Doria's accusations that had prompted it, of course. She'd made him doubt himself and his motivations for being here.

He wasn't so jaded that he'd discount her claim that his ego was involved. That had worried him, but as Raul said, regardless of why he was here, he *was* here. So why was Doria so determined to denigrate his efforts? Why did she refuse to help? That was the real mystery, because he had too many memories of her kissing the skinned knee of a sobbing toddler. Too many memories of her stealing a jar of peanut butter and giving it to someone she considered more unfortunate than herself, even though her stomach was growling from hunger pains. When he'd suggested she join the group, he'd expected her to jump at the chance. So, why hadn't she?

He kept hearing her say, "I want to fit in." He understood that need, but there came a time when you had to accept that living your life and fitting into society's mold weren't always compatible. When that happened, you were faced with hard choices.

He'd made his choices, and there had been times when he'd regretted them. On average, however, he knew that he'd done the right thing. Somehow, he had to make Doria see that by accepting who you were didn't make you less but more, because the more he thought about it, the more convinced he became that she'd refused to join the group because she was obsessed with her image.

"Matt, I need your help out here!" Raul called out frantically as a dozen boys surrounded him.

Matt laughed his first true laugh in more than two weeks as he tossed his towel aside. "You're a wimp, Raul."

"Save your insults for someone who cares," Raul replied as he tossed the ball toward Matt. "All I want is to turn this mad-dog crowd on someone else."

"Chicken!" Matt accused as he caught the ball and bounced it down the court with the boys hot on his heels.

Raul responded with an eloquent crow as he tucked his hands into his armpits and flapped his elbows. Matt started laughing so hard that the boys easily stole the ball away from him. He didn't care, because this was just a game. Doria, however, was a challenge, and he was ready to take her on.

DORIA DIDN'T KNOW why she was surprised by the size of Halliford's warehouse, which stretched the length of two city blocks. She had, after all, noted the immense size of their inventory. She supposed she'd been caught off balance because she found it difficult to believe that there was such a large market for their salacious merchandise. She liked sexy underwear as much as the next woman, but at least her undies didn't come in a plain brown wrapper.

Wilber Markham, Halliford's warehouse supervisor, was a small fidgety man with a badly receding hairline. He greeted them nervously, then took Matt aside. Doria walked over to a nearby stack of boxes, pretending to study them. Markham was clearly apprehensive about her visit, and she hoped Matt could calm him down. This was one part of her job she didn't like. The average person thought that an IRS agent was akin to an ogre or, in her case, an ogress.

"Are you ready to get started, Doria?" Matt finally asked.

"Yes," Doria answered, giving Markham a friendly smile. "I know that you're a busy man, Mr. Markham, and I promise to keep my visit as short as possible. I need to check some of your goods, but before I do that, could you show me how you enter and track your inventory?"

"Sure," he mumbled, casting an anxious glance toward Matt, who gave him an encouraging smile. "My office is in the back."

"Go easy on the man," Matt whispered as they followed him. "I think your visit has taken ten years off his life."

They entered Markham's office. The handful of clerical personnel seemed to be as jumpy at the sight of her as their boss had been. When she'd first started working for the IRS, she'd assumed this type of behavior was the result of a guilty conscience. But it had nothing to do with guilt—the mere mention of the IRS seemed to be enough to give even the most honest person heart palpitations.

She understood their reaction. Her agency had received some bad press over the years, but the cases reported in the media were the exception rather than the rule. Contrary to popular opinion, the IRS was only trying to ensure that everyone was paying their fair share of taxes. They weren't out to crucify anyone.

"This is Sandy Cox," Markham said, gesturing toward a plain, plump woman whom Doria guessed to be in her early twenties. "Sandy, this is Ms. Sinclair from the IRS. She has some questions about how we enter and track our inventory. Please show her what you do."

"I'm glad to meet you, Ms. Sinclair," Sandy answered.

"Please call me, Doria," Doria replied as she accepted the woman's hand. "And it's nice to meet you."

"So, what did you want to know?" Sandy asked.

"I would like to see how you track your inventory from the time you receive it until the time you ship it out."

"Okay." Sandy lifted a paper from a nearby stack and handed it to Doria. "We received this shipment last week. The block at the bottom shows the date it came in, the date that Receiving did a hand count to verify that the order was complete, and the date that the merchandise was placed into stock in the warehouse."

Doria studied the copy of a bill of lading. Since the merchandise had been shipped from the Orient, she checked specifically for the Customs clearance. Everything looked in order.

"When Receiving sends you the merchandise, how do you handle the paperwork?"

Sandy pointed to her computer. "We load it into Inventory and forward a copy of the bill of lading to Accounts Payable."

When you load the merchandise into Inventory, do you use the descriptions on the bill of lading?" Doria asked next.

"Yes."

Doria nodded. "How do you fill an order?"

"All the orders are received at the main office. They transmit it to us by computer. It prints out the shipping document, we fill the order and send it out."

"When your order comes in from the main office, does it come in by stock number and description, or just stock number?"

"Just stock number. It interfaces with our program, which already has the item descriptions."

"Thank you, Sandy. You've been a big help," Doria told her.

"That's all you want to know?" Sandy asked in disbelief.

"That's it."

Sandy and Markham exchanged stunned looks and Doria bit her inner cheek to keep from chuckling. She often felt as if people expected her to grill them under hot lights while smacking a rubber hose against her hand.

"Are you ready for the inspection?" Matt asked, causing Doria to jump.

She glanced over her shoulder and melted inside. Matt was standing so close that she could see the beginning shadow of beard along his jawline. Slowly, she raised her eyes to his slumberous green ones and melted even more. He had beautiful eyes, framed by long, thick lashes. A woman could easily get lost in them and never find her way out.

"Well?" he murmured huskily.

The deep, raspy sound of his voice vibrated through her, and it took several seconds for the meaning of his question to sink in.

"Yes. I'm ready for the inspection," she stated briskly when it did. She cursed the blush heating her cheeks. This certainly wasn't a professional way to behave in front of his client's employees!

"What did you want to see?" Markham asked, looking more relaxed.

"I have a list of stock numbers," Doria responded as she propped her briefcase on the edge of Sandy's desk and pulled out a sheet of paper.

Markham gulped as he looked at the list. "You want to inspect all of these items?"

"What is it, Mr. Markham?" Doria asked. It was evident the man was upset.

He blushed profusely. "It's nothing."

Sandy let out a derisive snort. "It is, too, something! Wilber's wife is pregnant and went into labor a couple of hours ago. He should be at the hospital. But the boss says he has to stick around until you're through with the inspection."

"That's ridiculous!" Matt exclaimed testily before Doria could respond. He grabbed Sandy's phone and began to dial. "I'll take care of this."

"No!" Markham yelped as he made a frantic lunge for the phone. "I can't afford to lose my job!"

"You're not going to lose your job," Matt said determinedly as he grabbed the phone off Sandy's desk and held it out of Markham's reach. When there was an answer on the other end, he barked, "This a Matt Cutter. Give me Henderson." Then, "I don't care if he's meeting with the president of the United States! Tell him if he doesn't want the IRS to throw his ass into jail, he'll get on the phone."

His threat worked, because he held the receiver away from his ear and winked at Doria as a voice began to screech at him.

"You're damn right you're in trouble," Matt growled when the voice on the other end lowered. "I have a lady treasury agent in your warehouse. She just found out that Markham's wife is at the hospital in labor and that he's been ordered to stay here until her inspection is over. Let me tell you, I'd rather be facing a swarm of killer bees than her right now. What the hell's wrong with you, Henderson? Women are hard enough to deal with, but when you start fooling around with their maternal instincts, you're asking for war."

The voice began to screech again, and Matt again pulled the receiver away from his ear. "Yeah, I hear you," he finally said. "Maybe you were just trying to be accommodating, but you blew it. If I were you, I'd get on the phone and send Markham to the hospital. By the way, this isn't his fault, and I sure hope that you don't have any plans to harass him. I have a feeling that this lady is going to keep tabs on him. If he loses his job, I can almost guarantee that you'll be audited both at work and at home until the day you die. If that happens, you can find yourself another accountant. I don't want to be on the IRS hit list.

"I'll try to calm her down," Matt said after a pause. "Just get Markham to the hospital. And Henderson? Just to prove that your heart is in the right place, why don't you give the man a raise? He does have a new mouth to feed." With that, he dropped the phone into place and grinned.

"'Women are hard enough to work with, but when you start fooling around with their maternal instincts, you're asking for war'?" Doria muttered dryly.

Matt had the good grace to look sheepish. "I know that was chauvinistic, but it was for a good cause, Doria."

"I'm going to lose my job," Markham mumbled to no one in particular.

The phone rang and Sandy grabbed it. "Yes, Mr. Henderson, Mr. Markham is right here."

Markham's hand shook as he took the receiver from her. "Yes, Mr. Henderson," he said. "Of course, Mr. Henderson. I know you didn't, Mr. Henderson. Why, thank you, Mr. Henderson. That's very generous."

He hung up and shook his head in disbelief. "I don't believe it. I'm going to get a raise!"

"Well, you can believe it later," Sandy said as she rose to her feet and bustled him toward the door. "Get to the hospital and take care of your wife. Call me when it's over. I don't care if it's three in the morning."

Markham nodded and then looked over at Doria and Matt. "By the way, what are your names?"

"Matt Cutter and Doria Sinclair," Matt answered.

"No, I mean your *names*. First and middle."

Matt and Doria exchanged confused looks.

"Matthew Peter," Matt replied.

"Doria Ann," Doria stated.

Markham gave them a huge smile. "Well, one of you should have a namesake by this time tomorrow. Thanks."

"I didn't know your middle name was Ann," Matt said when Markham disappeared.

Doria shrugged. "There are a lot of things you don't know about me."

Her statement hit Matt like a ton of bricks. Until this very moment, he would have sworn that he knew Doria almost as well as he knew himself. They'd been friends. *Best* friends. They'd confided in each other!

But that wasn't exactly true, Matt suddenly realized. He'd confided in Doria, but he couldn't fill one hand with the personal confidences she'd given him. He wanted to believe that it was because she'd chosen not to confide in him. When he thought about it, however, he recalled that one of the reasons he'd been so fond of Doria was because she'd been a good listener.

Had he really been that callow? he wondered, stricken by the revelation. Had he been so self-centered that he'd used their friendship as his own forum of self-expression? The only answer he could come up with was a resounding "Yes." No wonder she'd been able to let him take the fall so easily!

He was jolted away from his thoughts when Doria asked Sandy, "Do you have a map of the warehouse so we can perform our inspection?"

"You don't need a map," Sandy answered. "Everything's stocked in numerical order, and the numbers are listed on the aisle posts. I can go with you if you want."

"That won't be necessary," Doria said. "You have a lot of work to do. Thanks, though. You've been a big help."

"You're welcome, and if you need anything, just holler."

"We might need a box opener," Matt suggested.

"Oh! Of course." Sandy tugged open her drawer and handed him one. Then she gave them an impish grin. "Be careful out there. If you get lost, we might not find you until Christmas. This is a big warehouse."

"I'll leave a trail of bread crumbs," Doria responded with a chuckle. She glanced toward Matt. "Are you ready?"

"I've been ready all day," he drawled softly.

Doria had the distinct feeling that Matt wasn't talking about inspecting Halliford's goods.

"DAMMIT, DORIA, couldn't you have picked stock numbers that were at least in this country?" Matt grumbled fifteen minutes later when Doria checked the numbers on what seemed like the hundredth post and moved on.

"Halliford's your client," she grumbled back. "It's not my fault that their warehouse stretches to China."

"Are we at least getting close?" he asked as he tried to peer over her shoulder at her list of stock numbers.

"I thought we were close ten aisles back," she snapped, jerking the paper out of his sight. His closeness was grating on her nerves. His complaining was only making it worse. "You can leave, Matt. I've told you more than once that I can handle this inspection on my own."

"Maybe that's your problem, Doria. Maybe you do too many things alone."

"What's that supposed to mean?" She faced him, her stance defiant. She wasn't sure why she was so angry, other than she was so aware of him on a sexual level that she was about ready to explode.

"It means that you seem determined to do everything on your own. What's the big deal about letting someone help you once in a while?"

"You're not here to help, Matt. You're here to observe on behalf of your client. You're also here because I've allowed you to be here. I'm in charge, and you'd better not forget it!"

She was using that haughty tone again, and he fought for control of his temper. He wouldn't yell at her, but he wasn't going to take her threat lying down, either.

"And if I do forget, what are you going to do? Go after Halliford with both barrels loaded? I don't think so, Doria. You aren't that spiteful."

"Don't push your luck," she declared, heading for the next aisle. "Finally," she muttered when she spotted the number at the top of her list.

She headed down the aisle looking for the merchandise. She found it halfway down. The stock number was visible, but there was no description on the boxes, all of which were sealed.

"I guess this is where my help comes in," Matt said, waving the box opener at her. "Or would you rather have the honors? I don't want to step on any toes."

Doria gave him a withering look. "Just open the box."

He did as she instructed. When he looked inside, he cleared his throat and asked, "What's supposed to be in here?"

"The bill of lading says it's ladies' panties. The invoice says it's a chained thong. Which is it?"

"I think I'll let you make that determination."

Doria's jaw dropped when he turned to face her. Suspended between his hands was a scrap of sheer, red lace connected front to back by two thin gold chains on each side. The design was clearly meant to be a pair of women's panties, though Doria couldn't see why a woman would even bother to put them on. The fabric was so transparent it wouldn't provide any coverage.

"What's the verdict?" Matt drawled sexily.

Doria's gaze shot to his face and she blushed from head to toe when she saw that he was eyeing her hips avidly. The realization that he was imagining her dressed in that scrap of indecency sent a quiver of excitement rushing through her that was as shameless as the underwear.

"I think," she said coldly as she pivoted on her heel and walked away from him, "that I can cross off all references to panties versus thongs." She wanted to scream when he chuckled knowingly behind her.

They wandered down several more aisles before she came across another number on her list. She hesitated at the head of the aisle and glanced back the way they'd come. She could no longer see the office, and the deserted atmosphere was becoming eerily evident. She shivered and told herself that it was just the cool temperature in the warehouse. But if that was true, then why did she feel so feverish?

The answer, of course, was the six-foot-plus virile specimen of masculinity standing right behind her. She was tempted to ask Matt to wait here while she checked out the item in question. The bill of lading had said, Black Lace Teddy. The invoice had said Baring Surprise. She had a foreboding feeling that she was the one in for the surprise. She strode purposefully down the aisle, aware of Matt's matching steps behind her.

A box was open this time. She quickly delved a hand inside and pulled out the top item. When she held it up, she let out a strangled gasp of shock. It might be a black lace teddy, but the manufacturer had forgotten one essential piece. There was an underwire bustline, but there was no bra above it. No wonder they called it "Baring Surprise"!

"Now, that gives new meaning to going braless!" Matt exclaimed enthusiastically.

He made a grab for the undergarment before Doria could shove it back into the box. Her common sense told her not to look at him. In fact, it begged her not to look at him. Nevertheless, she slowly turned to face him.

Matt was holding the teddy by the spaghetti straps and studying it with a fervent intensity. Without warning, his gaze shot from the garment to Doria's chest. She was horrified to feel her nipples tightening beneath his scrutiny. When his eyes met hers, the message in their depths caused a primal response deep inside her.

Without a word, Matt took a step toward her. Doria, instinctively understanding his carnal intentions, backed away from him, shaking her head. He took another step toward her. She retreated again and jumped when her back came up against a pile of boxes. She knew she should be running for her life, but she couldn't tear her gaze away from his, let alone make her legs move. He had her mesmerized, hypnotized and bewitched.

"I want to touch you," he whispered in a voice so low, so erotic, that Doria's legs began to tremble.

He let the teddy drop to his feet and took hold of the fabric of her blouse where it tucked into the waistband of her slacks. With one quick jerk, he freed the tail and slid his hand beneath it.

Doria gasped softly as his hand caressed her waist and then began to move upward over her skin. His touch was electric and she was instantly damp with need. When his fingers touched the bottom of her bra, they traced it to the front clasp. He slid a finger over the metal clip and lightly stroked the valley between her breasts, his eyes never breaking his hold on hers.

"Will you let me touch you?" he rasped.

Doria knew that what he was asking was wrong, but she couldn't remember why. She gave a jerky nod.

His lips curved into a smile as he undid the clasp and slid his hand beneath the lace, cupping her breast. So slowly that it was almost painful, he let his thumb glide back and forth over her swollen nipple. Doria closed her eyes at the stimulating sensation that arrowed its way directly to her womb.

"Look at me," he ordered seductively. "I want to see how my touch makes you feel. I need to see that, honey. Open your eyes and look at me."

Doria's eyes opened slowly, and Matt groaned at the lustful glow in their depths. He'd never wanted a woman this badly, and yet that very need seemed to keep him connected with reality. He wanted to make love with her, but all he could do was touch her and, if she was willing, have her touch him.

He continued to cradle her breast with one hand as he popped open the snap on his pants and lowered the zipper with the other. Then he caught her hand and brought it to his abdomen. Even though he was anticipating her touch, his muscles jerked in response to the smoothness of her palm as it came into contact with his flesh. He held her hand against him, gazing deeply into her eyes, willing her to touch him. Then he released his hold on her hand, knowing that from here on out, what happened was up to her. He braced his forearm on the box beside her head and leaned toward her.

Doria instinctively stiffened when Matt caught her wrist and placed her hand against his belly. She told herself that touching him was wrong. She told herself that she had to pull away. So why was her hand drifting over him? Why did the feel of crisp male hair and smooth skin send tremors of excitement racing though her?

"Can I touch you?" she asked, unsure whether the weak, quavering voice speaking was her own.

"I thought you'd never ask," he murmured. "Oh, God, Doria!" he exclaimed lowly, roughly as she slid the tips of her fingers beneath the elastic of his shorts. When she delved even deeper, he heaved in a gulp of air, held his breath and closed his eyes. She was so close to touching his throbbing erection that he thought he would die if she didn't.

"Look at me," she whispered. "I need to see how my touch makes you feel."

Matt's eyelids instantly flew up as she used his own words against him. He slid his hand from her breast to her waist, tentatively toying with the zipper that rode on her hip.

"Go ahead," she urged throatily.

Matt didn't give her a chance to change her mind. He lowered her zipper and slipped his hand into her slacks. Her eyes widened and her chest heaved when he slid his hand across her concave stomach and slipped his fingers beneath the elastic of her panties. Everything male inside him was urging him to search deeper, but he waited for her next move.

"We shouldn't be doing this," she said tremulously. "I'm auditing your client."

Matt laughed weakly, unable to believe that she could even think about business at a time like this. "We can stop anytime you want. You're calling the shots, Doria."

A feeling of power shot through Doria at his words. She could say when to stop, and she only had to look into his eyes to know that no matter how far they went, if she did, he would.

"I want to touch you," she breathed.

"Then touch me," he urged.

"I . . . I want you to . . . touch me," she stammered hesitantly.

Matt nuzzled his nose against her cheek as it grew hot with embarrassment. "If that's what you want, then that's what I'll do."

Then he kissed her. He wanted to ravage her lips. Instead, he kissed her sweetly, gently, letting her take the lead. Letting her show him what she wanted. He nearly came unglued when her hand curled around his penis. His hand immediately went deeper.

He could feel her heat, her dampness, before he even touched her, and it was so erotic he peeled his lips from hers and rasped in her ear, "You feel so good, honey. So damn good."

"So do you! Oh, Matt, we shouldn't—"

Matt cut off her words by kissing her again. This time, he wasn't gentle. He was bold and aggressive. His tongue mimicked the action of his hips as he rocked himself in her hand. He hadn't forgotten her own need, and his fingers stroked her skillfully until he felt her shudder violently. The moment she climaxed, he shoved himself away and turned his back on her. He was so close to climax himself that he didn't know if he'd be able to regain control. He had to, however, because he wasn't about to embarrass Doria by walking out of the warehouse with a conspicuous stain on the front of his pants.

"Matt?" Doria whispered uncertainly as the fog began to clear. She felt the stirring of panic as she stared at his stiff posture.

"Everything's okay," he muttered tersely.

But Doria wasn't reassured. Why had he pulled away from her like that? Why was he refusing to face her? She felt confused and ashamed, and she quickly repaired her clothing. What had she done?

Her shame deepened, because she knew exactly what she'd done. She'd behaved like a schoolgirl groping with a boy in the back seat of a car. She'd never felt more humiliated in her life.

She bent to retrieve her papers from the floor. She didn't need to inspect any more of Halliford's stock. It was quite clear that the merchandise on the bills of lading and the invoices was the same. The only illegal activities going on in their warehouse were the ones that she and Matt were committing, and those were the most shameful acts of all.

"Doria, where are you going?" Matt yelled when he heard her take off running. He swung around just in time to see her disappear around the corner. "Damn!" he exclaimed as he went after her, zipping his pants as he ran.

He shouldn't have let things go so far. He shouldn't have— Hell, he had no regrets about what had happened between them, and she'd had control of the situation. She could have stopped them at any point. She *hadn't* said no.

Matt's legs were a lot longer than Doria's, but she'd had a good start on him. She'd already picked up her briefcase at the office and was running toward the exit by the time he caught up with her.

"Dammit, Doria, we have to talk," he said as he caught her arm and dragged her to a stop.

She yanked her arm out of his grasp and spun around to face him, her expression harsh and her eyes glittering with fury.

"Don't you dare touch me again, you...you pervert!" she spat.

Matt was so shocked by the loathing in her voice that she was gone before her departure even registered. When it did, his temper erupted. She'd called him a *pervert!* How dare she speak to him like that!

The more he thought about her attack, the madder he got. By the time he stormed out of the warehouse, he was angrier then he'd ever been in his life. Doria may have thought she'd had the last word, but she was wrong. He had no idea where she lived, but he was going to find her, even if he had to tear Los Angeles apart. Then he was going to have it out with her, once and for all!

# 7

"MY WORD, DORIA, what's wrong?" Kathy exclaimed in alarm when she opened her front door. "Are you sick?"

"Not physically," Doria answered dejectedly. Ever since she'd left Matt at the warehouse, she'd been driving around aimlessly. She hadn't even known she was headed for Kathy's until she'd stopped in front of her house. "I know I should have called before coming over, and if you're busy—"

"I'm never too busy for a friend," Kathy interrupted as she took a firm hold on Doria's arm and pulled her into the house. "You go into the den. I'll tell Herb not to disturb us."

"I don't want to interfere with your Friday night with your husband."

"Doria, you're not interfering. Herb has the cable sports channel on. He'll be glued to the television for hours. Go into the den. I'll be right back."

Doria did as instructed. As she wandered around Kathy's den, looking at all the family photographs, she thought about the past few hours. After leaving the warehouse, she'd been too upset to go to the office. She'd called in and told Dryer's secretary that she had some personal business to attend to and asked to be put down for two hours of vacation time.

She let out a short, ironic laugh. Dryer probably would never have learned that she'd taken those two hours off, but she hadn't been able to break the rules. Why couldn't she be as conscientious when it came to Matt?

Kathy entered with a tea tray. She placed it on the small coffee table centered between two wing chairs. "I was going to offer you a brandy, but I decided that since you're driving, tea would be better." She scrutinized Doria's face. "Of course, if you'd like to spend the night, we can forget the tea and hit the brandy bottle."

"I couldn't impose," Doria demurred.

"You're my friend, Doria, and friends aren't impositions," Kathy said in exasperation. "Besides, we now have three perfectly usable guest bedrooms. That's what happens when your kids fly the coop."

"Thanks, Kathy, but I couldn't possibly spend the night."

Kathy looked as if she might object but reached for the teapot instead. "Sit down, have a cup of tea and tell me why you're so upset."

"I've been sitting for hours. If you don't mind, I'd like to stand for a while."

"You can stand for as long as you want, but still have some tea."

Doria crossed the room and accepted the cup Kathy handed her, while asking herself why she was here. She couldn't discuss Matt with Kathy. The whole mess was too complicated and, quite frankly, too embarrassing.

"I'm sorry, Kathy," she said as she put the cup down and headed for the door. "I shouldn't have come. I'm sorry I bothered you."

"Doria, get back over here, sit down and tell me what's going on," Kathy ordered in a stern motherly voice that froze Doria in her tracks.

She turned around and stared at Kathy in disbelief. "Boy, talk about someone who cracks the whip."

"I didn't raise six kids for nothing," Kathy quipped. She pointed at the chair across from her. "Sit."

Doria wasn't sure why she obeyed. Perhaps it was because she'd never been faced with such parental authority. After she was seated, she folded her hands in her lap and said, "I don't know where to begin."

"Start by telling me why you're so upset."

"I can't. It's too humiliating," Doria replied, blushing profusely.

"Hmm," Kathy returned thoughtfully. "We must be talking about sex."

Doria's head shot up in dismay. "Is it that evident?"

Kathy chuckled. "No. I've just had to deal with a lot of these conversations over the years. I recognize the signs."

Doria slumped into the chair. "I've made the worst mistake of my life, and I don't know what to do about it. If Dryer ever finds out what's happened, I'll lose my job."

"So, you slept with your old friend?" Kathy guessed.

"Not exactly," Doria hedged.

"What kind of an answer is that? You either did or you didn't."

Doria propped her elbow on the arm of the chair and buried her face in her hand. "I can't talk about this."

"Well, I think you'd better talk about it so we can figure out what to do. Just tell me what happened. You can give me a thumbnail sketch of anything that's too embarrassing."

Doria hesitated, but plunged ahead. Once she started talking, the words tumbled out until she reached the point where Matt had asked to touch her. There she faltered, and no matter how hard she tried, she couldn't go on.

Kathy picked up where she left off. "Let me see if I can finish the story. The sexy underwear was a catalyst to the attraction between you and Matt. He looked at it, looked at you, and then you kissed?"

"Among other things," Doria confirmed, again burying her face in her hands. Kathy was silent for so long that Doria peeked through her fingers at her.

Suddenly Kathy's eyes widened in understanding. "I get the picture. You and he didn't make love, but you, uh..."

"Touched each other," Doria mumbled.

"Oh, dear." Kathy refilled her teacup and took a quick, nervous sip.

"I'm going to lose my job," Doria bemoaned.

"Oh, good heavens, Doria, stop being ridiculous," Kathy scolded. "Dryer is a stickler for the rules, but he is understanding. Go to him and explain that you and Matt are old friends who, after being reunited, discovered that there was a deep attraction. Tell him that you've fought against it, but you don't feel you can objectively handle the case."

"I can't do that!" Doria leaped out of the chair and began to pace around the room. "You know how Dryer is. He'll sense there's more and keep digging until he gets all the sordid details. Once he has them, he'll fire me."

Kathy was silent for several minutes before she said, "I still think you should go to Dryer, but I'll support you in this decision under one condition. I want you to promise that you'll let me review any decisions you make that might be questionable."

"I can't do that," Doria insisted. "If Dryer finds out that you've been covering for me, your job might be in jeopardy."

"I'm afraid that you'll have to take that chance," Kathy declared staunchly. "I can't stand by and let you continue on the audit without backup. You're my friend and I'd give you the shirt off my back, but if you don't let me help, then I'll have to go to Dryer myself."

With anyone else, Doria would have felt betrayed, but she knew that Kathy's words were not an act of betrayal. She wanted to help, but not at the risk of compromising their work. If their circumstances were reversed, Doria would have reacted the same way.

One part of Doria wanted to leap at her friend's offer. The other part insisted that it was too reminiscent of when she'd let Matt take the fall.

"I need to think this over, Kathy," she said. "I'll give you my decision Monday."

DORIA WAS ALMOST to the security gate of her apartment building when she saw a man move in the shadows. Her first response was a flash of panic. Her neighborhood was quiet and respectable, but no neighborhood was completely safe these days.

She forced herself to stay calm and gauged the distance between herself and the gate. She could probably make it, but she didn't think she could get it unlocked before he was upon her. A dash to her car was out of the question. Even if she could outrun him, she'd still have to unlock the door.

Left with no other option, she prepared herself for combat. In the old days, she'd fought off more than one assailant, and though her techniques were rusty, she was sure they'd serve her well. She took a firm grip on her computer and briefcase and continued to walk toward the gate, pretending not to notice the man. If he thought he was catching her by surprise, he'd be off guard. She could take him before he realized what was happening.

When he stepped into her path, she didn't even look at him. She swung her briefcase at his head, while kicking violently toward his groin.

"Dammit, Doria, I know you're mad at me, but that's no reason to unman me!" Matt roared as he leaped backward, barely managing to escape her assault.

"Matt?" she gasped, momentarily stunned to see him standing in front of her. Then her temper erupted. "What do you think you're doing creeping up on me like that?"

"Just calm down," he muttered irritably. If his reflexes hadn't been so finely honed, he shuddered to think what she would have done to him. He'd once determined that it would be a mistake to underestimate her fighting ability. He'd almost learned the hard way that he'd been right. "I didn't mean to frighten you."

"If you didn't mean to frighten me, then why were you slinking around in the shadows? Dammit, Matt, for an intelligent man, you sure do some stupid things."

"I'm sorry," he said solemnly, though his lips were twitching. He decided he liked Doria in a rage. She looked sexy as hell. "I want to talk about what happened today. I was afraid that if you saw me waiting, you'd turn tail and run."

Doria's anger fled and was replaced by embarrassment. He'd had her so rattled that she'd forgotten the humiliating scene at the warehouse.

"We have nothing to talk about," she stated stiffly.

"We have a lot to talk about," he corrected. "I know you regret what happened, and I regret it, too, but—"

"As I said, we have nothing to talk about," Doria interrupted curtly, stung by his words. She circled around him and walked toward the gate. She did regret what had happened, so why did it hurt so badly to learn that he felt the same way? "Go home, Matt."

*Damn, the woman was stubborn!* Matt fumed as he followed her. "I'm not going home. We're going to talk. We need to clear the air."

"As far as I'm concerned, the air is cleared." She unlocked the security gate and held it open with her shoulder as she looked at him. "What happened today should have never happened. I'm going to forget it, and I'm sure you'll have no trouble doing the same."

"You're some piece of work," Matt muttered as he grabbed the gate and pushed her through it. When they were in the courtyard, he stood facing her, his hands jammed into his pockets and his shoulders hunched. "You might try to forget what happened, but you aren't going to be able to do it any more than I am. We have to talk this out. If we don't, it's going to happen again."

Doria glared at him. "There is nothing to talk about, and I can guarantee that it *won't* happen again. You can make a fool out of me once, Matt, but you'll never do it a second time. Now, please leave. You're in a security building uninvited."

With that, she headed across the courtyard to her apartment, aware of Matt's eyes boring into her back. Her hands were shaking, but she managed to get her key in the first lock. By the time she went to work on the second one, Matt was bearing down on her. He reached her just as she opened the door.

"I wasn't trying to make a fool out of you," he said quietly. "Let me talk to you, Doria. Please."

She leaned her forehead against the doorjamb and repeated by rote, "There's nothing to talk about."

"Maybe you don't have anything to say, but I do. Give me five minutes, and then I promise to leave."

Doria's common sense told her to give him an unequivocal no, but she came to the conclusion that if she didn't give him his five minutes now, he'd force her to give them to him at his office. At least here, they'd be alone. There, they always had Uless for an audience.

"All right," she conceded wearily. "You have five minutes."

"Thank you, Doria."

"Yeah." She walked into her apartment, stopping at the small entryway closet to store her briefcase and computer.

Matt entered, closed the door and surveyed her living room. There were only a few pieces of furniture—a sofa, a coffee table, a portable television and a small stereo—but the pieces had an understated elegance that declared they were expensive. It wasn't that Matt was turned off by the room. It was very pretty, if you liked "pretty."

"Your apartment's nice," he said.

"Thank you, but that isn't why you're here," Doria replied. "Your five minutes have started. Please say what you have to say. I have a lot to do this evening."

Matt ignored her and strode farther into the room. He studied the knickknacks in the small built-in bookcase next to the sofa. There were several unicorns, a few griffins, and a couple of dragons. He found it interesting that she collected mythical beasts. Never in a million years would he have guessed that she could be so whimsical.

"Matt, your time is running out." Doria shifted from one foot to the other. She didn't like him prowling through her apartment.

He swung toward her suddenly and asked, "Why did you run away this afternoon?"

"If that's what you're here to talk about, forget it."

"I'm not going to forget it. I think I know why you fled, but I want you to confirm it."

"Why? So you can humiliate me further?"

"I never meant to humiliate you." He walked to her and stopped when he was only inches away.

"Don't lie to me, Matt," she said, slashing her hand through the air. "It was bad enough that we did what we did, but when you—"

She clamped her mouth shut when she realized she'd been ready to confess how hurt she'd been by his rejection. She'd never admit that to him. Never!

"When I what?" he prodded. She didn't answer, so he said, "You're upset because you did something you consider out of character. What we did may have been racy, considering where we were, but there was nothing perverted about it, Doria. It was good, wholesome sex."

Doria gave a disgusted shake of her head. "Come on, Matt, be honest with yourself. You were turned on by a handful of lascivious underwear. I just happened to be handy enough for you to sate your lust."

"Sate my lust?" he repeated incredulously. He grabbed her hand and pressed it against the front of his trousers. "Does that feel as if my lust was sated?"

"Don't be crude," she snapped as she jerked her hand away and rubbed it against her thigh. She'd had enough humiliation for one day. *No, make that enough for one lifetime.*

"I'm not being crude," Matt stated between clenched teeth. His temper was stirring and he refused to lose it. He was going to make her see reason if it took him all night.

"That's a matter of opinion," she stated disdainfully. "Your five minutes are up. I'd appreciate it if you'd leave."

Her haughty tone was Matt's undoing. She was absolutely, positively maddening. He wanted to shake her and kiss her at the same time. He took a purposeful step toward her.

"Matt, you said you'd leave after five minutes," Doria reminded uneasily as she took two steps backward.

He took another step toward her. "I lied."

"You don't lie," Doria noted anxiously, but her anxiety wasn't caused by him. That damnable hot and reckless feeling was surfacing. How could he keep doing this to her?

"You always tell the truth. You also never break a promise, and you promised you'd leave."

"Well, as they say, there's a first time for everything." His eyes dropped to her breasts, and he smiled in satisfaction when he saw her nipples pressing against the fabric of her prim and proper blouse. She was as turned-on as he was. He raised his gaze to her face. "I want you, Doria."

"Well, I don't want you!" she responded shrilly as she backed up several more steps. She stumbled against the coffee table, lost her balance and sat down on it—hard. She gripped the edges as Matt continued to advance. When he came to a stop in front of her, she said, "I'm not going to play this game with you, Matt. You've already rejected me once."

"When have I ever rejected you?" he demanded, taken aback by her accusation.

She ducked her head, but not quickly enough to hide the hurt in her eyes. "This afternoon."

Matt caught her chin and forced her to look at him. "What are you talking about?"

Color flooded her face. "You turned away from me after we, uh, you know."

Matt would have laughed if she hadn't looked so wretched. "I wasn't rejecting you. I was a breath away from ejaculation. If I hadn't pulled away, I would have walked out of the warehouse with a very obvious stain on the front of my pants. I didn't think you'd appreciate having the whole world know that we'd been doing more than inspecting goods at Halliford."

Her blush deepened, and Matt knew she was embarrassed. When she tried to pull away from him, he held her in place. He stroked his thumb across her hot cheek. "There's nothing to be ashamed of, Doria."

She glared at him. "That's easy for you to say. What have you got to lose? Not your job, and certainly not your reputation. You're a man. You're supposed to put notches on your bedpost."

"Now who's being crude?" he admonished. "I don't put notches on my bedpost and never have. Your problem is that you're obsessed with your image. You have this perfect picture of yourself in your mind. That picture cracked today, because you suddenly realized that you want to be just as crude as you claim I am. You want to touch me and have me touch you. You want to make love with me. I think I should give you what you want."

"No," Doria said with a vehement shake of her head.

Matt dropped to his knees in front of her, and then sat back on his heels. When they were at eye level, he said, "Look me in the eye and tell me you don't want to make love with me, Doria. Make me believe it."

"I don't—" Doria began, but her words died when Matt grabbed the hem of his T-shirt, stripped it over his head and tossed it aside. She told herself to look away. She told herself that she wasn't interested in his magnificent chest, which was more muscular and hairier than she'd imagined. She might even have believed herself if her gaze hadn't been drawn to that fine pink scar that ran from his left breast to the bottom of his rib cage. The fact that he'd been hurt made her ache unbearably. She wanted to touch the scar, to run her lips over it.

"Well, Doria?" Matt taunted as he rubbed his hand across his chest and then let it follow the narrow line of hair down his abdomen to his waist. He popped open the snap of his jeans. "Do you remember what it was like to touch me?"

"No," Doria moaned, shutting her eyes tightly. But it didn't wipe out the image of him sitting there in half-naked splendor. "Go away."

"Is that really what you want?" he asked huskily. He propped his hands on the edge of the table and leaned toward her. "If it is, I'll leave, but you're still going to have to look me in the eye and tell me to go."

"Why are you doing this to me?" she cried.

"Because I want to shower you with kisses from head to toe. Because I want to touch you and watch you come to life. Because I want to be inside you and experience your softness and your heat. Because I want to watch your face when you climax, and I want to join you in that euphoria. Then I want to hold you in my arms and tell you what it was like for me. I want to hear what it was like for you. I want it all, Doria. But I'll go away if you just look me in the eye and tell me that you don't want the same things."

Doria heaved a deep breath and told herself that that was exactly what she was going to do: open her eyes and tell him she didn't want any of those things, even if it was a bald-faced lie. She'd been lying for years now. How hard would it be to give him the words?

It wasn't hard—it was impossible, she realized when she forced her eyes open and found herself drowning in his green-eyed gaze. All the desire that had been building over the weeks hit her with a staggering force.

"I want you," she whispered hoarsely.

He gave her a smile that was both triumphant and tender as he sat back on his heels and spread his arms wide. "Then come get me, honey."

Doria launched herself into his arms.

MATT HAD SUSPECTED that beneath Doria's prim exterior beat the heart of a seductress. He was still stunned when she wrapped her arms around his neck and kissed him wantonly. He became so aroused that he was trembling from head to toe, and he fell back on the floor, bringing her over him. She let out a meow of pleasure as she straddled his hips and stroked herself against his erection. Her hands were flying over his chest, treating him to soft, tantalizing caresses that were so stimulating, he became feverish with desire.

He was desperate to touch her as she was touching him. Without releasing her lips, he went to work on the buttons on her blouse. Then he popped open the front clasp of her bra and stripped the garments down her arms. He groaned when he returned to her breasts. They fit perfectly in his palms, and he brushed his thumbs over her swollen nipples. He was rewarded by another meow of pleasure. When she placed her hands on his chest and mimicked him by brushing her thumbs over his nipples, he nearly lost it.

He caught her rocking hips to hold her still and broke away from the kiss, whispering tautly, "Slow down, honey. My control is about to snap."

Doria's mind was so muddled by passion that she couldn't make sense of his words. All she knew was that he was withdrawing from her again, and she wasn't going to let him do it. She unzipped his pants and slid her hand inside, stroking him boldly.

Matt's response was an earthy curse as he rolled her to her back. "Birth control?" he rasped as he jerked down the zipper of her slacks and began to shove them down her legs. Her panty hose and panties quickly followed. "Do I need it?"

Doria shook her head as she kicked her legs free of her clothing. She couldn't speak. She couldn't think. All she wanted was for Matt to take her—here, now and as fast as he could. He slid out of his pants. A moment later he was hovering over her, his forearms braced on either side of her head.

"Are you sure this is what you want?" he grated. "If it isn't, then tell me now, honey. In a couple of seconds, I won't be able to back off."

Doria wrapped her arms around his neck and kissed him as she parted her thighs in welcome. With an expressive groan, he thrust into her deeply and completely. She gasped at his entry. He felt so good inside her. He made her feel so complete.

"Everything okay?" he rasped in her ear.

"Make love to me," she rasped back as she wrapped her legs around his waist.

"I'm not going to be able to hold back," he forewarned as he began an urgent rhythm that hurled him toward climax. "I've wanted you for too long."

Doria didn't even attempt to respond. He had her flying and she clung to him as she approached the zenith. When she hit it, it rocked her to the core.

Matt immediately followed her to fulfillment. He was still shuddering with the bliss of release as he collapsed against her. When he was finally able to catch his breath, he raised his head and stared at her face. Her eyes were closed, and her hair was in wild disarray. He'd never seen her look more beautiful.

When several seconds passed and she didn't open her eyes, he became concerned. "Are you okay, honey?" His concern turned to alarm when a single tear crept from beneath her lashes and rolled down her cheek. "Doria, what is it? Did I hurt you?"

*Hurt me?* Doria repeated on a silent, bitter wail. Yes, she was hurting, but not in the way he meant. Now that she and Matt had made love, she was going to have to go to Dryer and turn in her resignation. How was she going to make a living? How was she going to take care of her father?

"Oh, God, Doria, I'm sorry," Matt murmured remorsefully when a tear rolled down her other cheek. "I didn't mean to hurt you."

The anguish in his voice broke through Doria's bout of self-pity. After Monday, she'd have plenty of time to feel sorry for herself. Right now, she had to reassure Matt.

She opened her eyes and gave him what she hoped was an encouraging smile. "You didn't hurt me. I hurt myself." She sighed at his perplexed expression, knowing that she was going to have to explain. "By making love with you, I've crossed over the line. I have no option but to go to my boss on Monday and resign before he has a chance to fire me."

"Resign?" he repeated in disbelief as he sat up. "Come on, Doria. You can't quit your job because we've made love!"

"It's either that or be fired," she said as she sat up beside him.

"That's ridiculous. The only way your boss would know what's happened is if you tell him, and you won't tell him."

"I have to tell him," she insisted stubbornly.

"No, you don't." He gripped her upper arms and gave her a gentle shake. "You don't destroy everything you've worked for because of one indiscretion, Doria. I'll admit that we shouldn't have made love tonight, but I swear to you that it won't happen again as long as you're doing the audit." When she looked skeptical, he said, "We can do it, Doria. I know we can."

"And what if we can't?" she challenged. "What do we do if this happens again?"

"We'll find a way to release the tension so it won't happen again."

Doria's responding laugh bordered on hysteria. She climbed to her feet and headed for her bedroom, saying, "And how are we supposed to do that? Kiss? That's against the rules. Hug? That's against the rules. *Everything* is against the rules!"

Matt jumped up and followed her. "We'll figure out something. Just don't go off half-cocked and resign from your job."

Doria was tempted to listen to him, because she was torn by her need to be honest with her boss and her need to preserve her reputation and her livelihood. As she grabbed her robe and pulled it on, she almost convinced herself that Matt was right—that they could find a way to release the tension without making love. But then she looked at him. He was standing in the doorway, oblivious to his nudity; she wasn't oblivious, though.

She gave an incredulous shake of her head. "You're aroused."

He shrugged. "I said I wouldn't make love to you. I didn't say I'd stop wanting you."

"But we just made love!"

"Sometimes it happens that way." His eyes shifted from her to her unmade bed and he released a sigh of regret. "I think I'd better get out of here. Otherwise, I'm likely to tumble you onto those rumpled sheets and make love to you all night."

Doria shivered at the images his words provoked. She had to forcefully push them away. "Yes, I think you'd better leave."

He searched her face. "You're not going to do anything rash about your job, right?"

"Right," Doria lied, because she knew that if she didn't, he wouldn't leave, and she had to get him out of here. She'd just realized that she was hopelessly in love with him, which meant that she could no longer be objective when it came to Halliford. She would have to give Dryer her resignation. If she let Matt stay, he might convince her otherwise.

"Good girl," Matt said. Then he walked back into the living room.

Doria stayed in the bedroom while he dressed. When he called out that he was ready to leave, she reluctantly joined him.

"I suppose a good-night kiss is out," he commented when she walked him to the door.

"It's against the rules," she agreed, forcing a bright smile.

He skimmed his fingers across her cheek. "Tell me you don't have any regrets."

"I don't have any regrets," she repeated dutifully.

"You don't know how relieved that makes me feel." He dropped a quick kiss on her forehead. "Sweet dreams, honey."

Doria watched him walk across the courtyard. When he started through the gate, he turned and waved, and she waved back. It was only when the gate closed behind him that her tears began to fall.

She brushed at them impatiently as she closed the door. She didn't have time to cry. She had to decide where she'd go after she handed Dryer her resignation. She couldn't stay in L.A. Matt was here, and she had to get as far away from him as possible.

How could she have let herself fall in love with him again? Was this her punishment for betraying him? She also had no idea how she was going to support herself, and the nursing-home costs for her father were going to increase next month. She'd never be able to use Dryer as a reference, which meant she wouldn't be able to work in the accounting field. Ten years of hard work had just gone up in smoke because she'd lost control of her libido. Had making love with Matt been worth losing everything?

Yes, she decided, as she wandered back into her bedroom and fell across her bed. Heaven help her, yes.

# 8

DORIA KNEW that her boss came to work an hour before anyone else, and she was waiting for him when he arrived. She hoped to give him her resignation, clean out her desk and be gone before the majority of her coworkers came in.

When Dryer took one look at her and said, "Go into my office, Doria. I'll get us some coffee," she recognized her efforts to camouflage her sleepless weekend had been for naught. His offer was significant, because he normally considered getting coffee women's work. Thankfully she'd had the foresight to put on a pot, so her wait was short. When he returned, he handed her a mug and rounded his desk.

Doria took an obligatory sip before setting the mug aside. Then she leaned forward and placed an envelope on his desk. "I need to talk with you, Mr. Dryer, but before I tell you what's happened, I'd like to say that this is my resignation. It'll save you from having to fire me."

Dryer arched a brow. "I see."

When nothing more was forthcoming from him, she leaned back in her chair, folded her hands in her lap and began.

"Halliford's accountant is a childhood friend. We hadn't seen each other since I was fourteen. When you gave me the file, I thought there might be a problem. He'd moved, and when he left we weren't on the, uh, best of terms."

She paused and Dryer nodded for her to continue. She had to clear her throat before she could comply. "Well, I was right. We did have a problem, but we agreed to declare a truce until the audit was over. Then, we discovered that we were attracted to each other." She glanced down at her hands. "To make a long story short, Friday night we made love."

"I see," Dryer murmured again as he rose to his feet and crossed to the window. He stared out as he linked his hands behind his back. Finally, he said, "Friday night was the first time this had happened?"

"Yes," Doria answered. She wasn't lying, she told herself. What had happened in the warehouse wasn't really lovemaking.

"Has anything like this happened to you on previous audits?" he asked.

"Absolutely not!" Doria exclaimed, aghast at the question.

He gave her a conciliatory smile. "Forgive me for asking, Doria, but under the circumstances I felt it was necessary."

Doria blushed and glanced back down at her hands. "I understand, but I swear to you that nothing like this has ever happened before."

"I believe you." He returned to his desk. "You know that this is a serious infraction."

"That's why I'm tendering my resignation."

"Well, I'm not going to accept it."

"But you have to!" Doria cried as her head shot up. "I don't want to be fired."

"I'm not going to fire you, Doria. What you did was wrong, but I respect you for coming to me right away instead of trying to cover it up. You're a conscientious employee, and today you proved that. I don't want to lose you. I will, of course, have to take you off the Halliford audit."

He flipped through the work schedule on his desk. "Andy Cross just became available. Please gather together everything you've done on the audit so I can give it to him."

"I've already put everything together," Doria answered weakly, still reeling from the realization that she wasn't going to be standing in the unemployment line. She couldn't decide if she was pleased or dismayed by this unexpected turn of events. The office would be rife with speculation about why she'd been pulled off the audit. Knowing that she would be the brunt of gossip was almost worse than being fired.

"Good. All that's left for us to do is to notify Halliford's accountant that another agent will be taking over. Do you want to call him?"

"No!" Doria responded sharply. She blushed when she realized how shrill she'd sounded, but she'd already resolved that she'd never see or speak to Matt again. Just because she wasn't going to be leaving town didn't change that decision. "I would prefer that you tell him."

"Fine. Give me his name and number when you bring in the rest of the paperwork."

"Do you have another audit for me?" she asked hopefully. If she could get back in the field, she wouldn't have to face her coworkers.

Her shoulders slumped in resignation when he said, "Not right now, but I should have something next week."

"In that case, would it be all right if I took the rest of the week off?" If she couldn't hide out on an audit, then she could hide out at home.

"Of course," he agreed with an understanding smile.

Doria rose to her feet. "Thank you. I'll go get that paperwork."

She was getting ready to leave the office when Kathy arrived. Kathy took one look at her and said, "You've told Dryer about you and Matt."

"I had to tell him," Doria responded with a heavy sigh. "Matt was waiting for me when I got home Friday night, and . . ."

"You don't have to say any more," Kathy stated when Doria's voice trailed off. "I get the picture."

Doria gave a disheartened shake of her head. "I've worked so hard to earn people's respect around here, and now they're all going to be talking about me. At least I won't be around to listen to the whispers," she concluded as she grabbed her briefcase and stood.

"Dryer fired you?" Kathy gasped in disbelief.

"He wouldn't even accept my resignation," Doria told her ruefully. "He gave me the week off to pull myself together."

"Thank heavens," Kathy said as she clapped her hand to her chest. "You almost gave me a heart attack. I told you that he isn't an unfeeling brute."

"No, he's not. He was very civilized about the entire mess."

"Well, you go home and get some rest," Kathy ordered as she gave her a one-armed hug. "And don't worry about the gossipmongers. Only Dryer and me know what's happened, and we won't say a word."

"Thanks," Doria said, forcing a smile. She knew Kathy meant to reassure her, but it didn't work. "I'll see you in a few days."

"Take care, kid, and if you need anything, call me."

"Yeah," Doria replied as she hurried toward the door.

She promised herself she wouldn't cry until she got home, and somehow she managed to uphold that vow. The minute she stepped into her apartment, however, the tears came with such force that she barely managed to shut the door and lock it. Unable to take another step, she sank to the floor, buried her face in her hands and began to sob. All she'd ever wanted was to live her life like a normal person. So how had everything gotten so darned screwed up?

MATT COULDN'T BELIEVE that his first appointment was at nine, with a potential new client. That was the time Doria usually arrived, and he wanted to speak with her the moment she walked in the door. She'd told him that she wouldn't do anything foolish, but he had an ominous presentiment that all hell was about to break loose.

Of course, his appointment, Sara Howard—a middle-aged woman who had recently opened a bookstore—arrived fifteen minutes early. Matt was tempted to make her wait until after Doria arrived but squelched the urge. Ms. Howard had made an early appointment so she could open her store on time. He owed it to her to be accommodating. He tried to listen to what she was saying, but when nine o'clock came and went and he hadn't heard the outer door open, he gave up.

"I'm sorry, Ms. Howard," he said, interrupting her in midsentence. "I'm afraid that my mind is on a personal problem and I'm having trouble concentrating. Could we meet another day? I'll be happy to come to the bookstore, and, of course, I'll understand if you choose to use another accountant."

"But I don't want another accountant," she informed him. "You're supposed to be the best, and I want the best."

Matt smiled. "Thank you for the compliment, and I'm sure we can work something out. May I give you a call later in the week?"

"Sure. I know how personal matters can prey on the mind. I hope it's nothing serious."

"I hope so, too," Matt replied as he stood and escorted her to the door. When she was gone, he turned on Uless. "Any word from Doria?"

"In a roundabout way," Uless answered. "Her boss called. Ms. Sinclair will no longer be working on the Halliford audit. Mr. Andrew Cross will replace her as of tomorrow."

Matt slammed his fist against his palm. "I should have known she'd do this. She's so damn ethical!"

"I thought you admired ethics."

"I do, but not when you use them to cut your nose off to spite your face. If she's resigned, I'll . . . Hell, I don't know what I'll do, but I'll do something."

"Resigned?" Uless repeated as he straightened in his chair and eyed Matt avidly. "Why would she resign?"

"That's none of your business. Do we have a number for her office?"

"Right here." Uless extended the phone message.

Matt snatched it out of his hand and hurried into his office. He dialed the number and glanced up to see Uless lounging in the doorway. He started to tell him to leave, but the phone was answered on the other end.

When he asked for Doria, the woman said, "I'm sorry, but Ms. Sinclair is not in. Perhaps her boss can help you. He's taking her calls."

Matt cursed. If her boss was taking her calls, did that mean she'd resigned, or that she was on another audit?

"No, her boss can't help me," he told her. "This is an urgent personal matter. Can you tell me how to reach her?"

"Oh, dear," the woman murmured. "I hope it isn't one of her parents."

That drew Matt up short. What was she talking about? Doria's parents were dead. He decided, however, that he'd use her concern to his advantage.

"As a matter of fact, it's her, uh, father. I need to speak with Doria as soon as possible. Do you know where I can reach her?"

"At home, I suppose. Do you have that number?"

"Yes, I do. Thanks." He dropped the receiver into place and buried his face in his hands.

"Bad news?" Uless asked with a snap of his gum.

"She can be reached at home and her boss is taking her calls. She's definitely resigned, and it's all my fault."

"I suppose you want me to reschedule as many of your appointments as possible," Uless stated pragmatically.

"Why didn't you tell me you were clairvoyant?" Matt replied as he reached for the phone and dialed Doria's home number.

He let it ring twenty-five times before finally giving up. Either she was out or she wasn't answering. The only way to find out for sure was to go to her apartment.

Uless managed to reschedule all of Matt's appointments but two. Both people were already on their way. Luckily, they required simple tasks that Matt could have performed with his eyes closed. While he worked, he had Uless call Doria's number every five minutes. It was after eleven before he could leave. Doria still hadn't answered.

"Maybe she's taken a trip," Uless suggested.

Matt shook his head. "She wouldn't take a trip if she's out of work. She's too practical for that. I just hope that she hasn't loaded up a moving van and taken off for parts unknown."

"You really care about her," Uless said.

"I think I'm in love with her," Matt confessed grimly as he headed for the door. Being in love with Doria wasn't going to be easy. She had a propensity for driving him crazy. "Hold down the fort, Uless, and be sure to turn on the answering machine before you leave for school."

"I've got you covered. Good luck with the lady treasury agent."

"Thanks. I have a feeling I'm going to need all the luck I can get."

WHEN THE INTERCOM BUZZER went off, Doria knew it was Matt. She ignored it and huddled deeper into the corner of her overstuffed sofa. She wasn't going to see him. She had to end things between them before she got in any deeper.

There was no future for her and Matt, she told herself firmly. He worked in the ghetto because he didn't want to let go of his roots. She'd pulled hers up and had no intention of replanting them. He lived in a neighborhood that used a gang as their "neighborhood watch" program. She lived in an apartment building with a security gate. He dressed in denim and leather and rode a motorcycle. She dressed for success and hoped to someday own a BMW convertible. The only thing they had in common was their work, and even that was on the opposite end of the spectrum. So, why was she in love with him? It was the riddle of the century.

She nearly fell off the sofa when her doorbell rang. He'd somehow made it through the security gate. She didn't know why she was surprised. He was Matt, after all, and what he set out to do, he usually accomplished.

She pressed her hands to her ears when he leaned on the bell. When he started pounding on the door and calling out her name, she knew that if she didn't answer, she'd probably be evicted. The building manager had no sense of humor.

With a resigned sigh, she climbed off the sofa and walked to the door. The way she had it figured, Matt would take one look at her and leave. She'd cried all morning, and she was not a pretty crier. Her eyes practically swelled shut. Her nose turned red, and her skin became blotchy.

She no more than cracked open the door when Matt pushed his way inside. Before she could utter a word, he swept her into his arms.

"Oh, honey, I've been so worried about you," he whispered harshly.

Doria levered her head back and stared up at him. "As you can see, I'm fine, so you can leave."

"Leave?" he repeated disbelievingly. "I'm not going to leave you at a time like this, and— My God, Doria, what have you done to yourself? You look like death warmed over a half-dozen times!"

"I've been crying," she said with a sniff as she tried to extricate herself from his embrace. He only tightened his hold on her.

"Oh, honey." He buried his face in her hair. "Why didn't you call me? I would have been here for you. And you don't have to worry about a thing. You can work with me. My business is getting to the point where I'm going to need some help, and your expertise would be invaluable."

"What are you talking about?" Doria asked as she tried again to break out of his embrace. She'd have had better luck battling her way out of a straitjacket.

He finally eased his stranglehold on her enough to where she could lean back in his arms. "I'm talking about your job. I know you resigned today, and—"

"I didn't resign," she interrupted impatiently.

"You mean you were fired? No wonder you've been crying your eyes out!"

"I wasn't fired, either," she muttered as she pushed against his chest. "Let me go, Matt. Right now!"

He released her so quickly she nearly fell. She stumbled back several steps and glowered at him when she finally managed to regain her balance. To her amazement, he was glowering right back.

"You weren't fired?" he questioned tightly.

"No."

"Then you did resign."

She shook her head.

"Then what in hell happened this morning?" he bellowed.

Doria's eyebrows soared in astonishment. Why was he angry? She was the one who'd been to hell and back. "I went to my boss and told him we'd made love. I offered him my resignation, but he refused to accept it."

"Then why are you crying? Dammit, Doria, to look at you, you'd think the world had ended!"

"My world has ended!" she yelled at him, incensed by his insensitivity. "I've spent years building a respectable image. *Years,* Matt! Now I'm fodder for the office gossip-mill, and all because I had the bad taste to make love with a Neanderthal like you!"

The moment the words were out of her mouth, she wanted to snatch them back. Matt's thunderous expression told her she'd gone too far. She backed up hurriedly when he took a purposeful step toward her.

"I didn't mean that the way it sounded, Matt." He didn't respond, but continued to advance on her. She held her hands up, palms extended. "Please, Matt. Don't overreact. I really didn't mean it that way."

"There's only one way to interpret the meaning of Neanderthal, Doria. If I'm a caveman, then maybe I should act like one."

She scrambled quickly out of his way when he lunged for her. "Matt, I was angry. I said the first thing that was guaranteed to infuriate you. I'm sorry!"

She heaved a sigh of relief when he stopped stalking her. Then she frowned when he fished a pack of cigarettes out of the pocket of his T-shirt. "When did you start smoking?"

"Twelve years ago. I've had a bet with Uless on which one of us could stop smoking, so I haven't been smoking for the past month."

He peeled off the cellophane and Doria cleared her throat. "You don't intend to smoke here, do you?"

His brows drew together in a scowl. "Don't tell me you're one of those nonsmoking freaks?"

"No. I'm one of those allergic freaks. Cigarette smoke makes me deathly ill. If you want to smoke, that's fine with me, but you'll have to take it outside."

"You're kidding me," Matt stated incredulously. "It really makes you sick?"

Doria nodded vigorously. "It really makes me sick. I throw up and get migraine headaches."

"I can't believe this." He eyed the pack of cigarettes longingly. He'd bought it on the way over because he'd remembered what it had been like waiting for Doria on Friday night. He'd decided that if she was gone, then he needed something to occupy him while he waited for her to come home. Besides, his month was up and he'd never managed to quit smoking for longer than a month.

It was as if Doria read his mind, because she said, "If you haven't had a cigarette for a month, then the nicotine is out of your system. That means that your need for one is psychological. Have you considered behavior modification?"

Matt looked at her askance. "I don't want to modify my behavior. I want a cigarette."

"Then maybe you should consider aversion therapy," Doria replied, warming to the subject. "I used that to solve my craving for ice cream. I ate nothing but ice cream for two weeks, and now I can hardly stand the sight of the stuff."

"Are you suggesting I eat these?" Matt asked, holding up the pack.

"No, you should chain smoke until the pack is empty. In fact, you should probably chain-smoke an entire carton of cigarettes."

She walked over to him, grabbed his arm and led him to the door. She couldn't believe that she'd stumbled upon such a brilliant strategy to get rid of him.

"Believe me, Matt, it will work. Just hurry to the nearest store, buy yourself a carton of cigarettes and then lock yourself into a closed room. Don't even open a window, so you'll get the full impact of the smoke."

They'd reached the door and she twisted the doorknob, but when she pulled, the door wouldn't open.

"You're not going to get rid of me that easily," Matt drawled softly.

Doria glanced up and realized that the door wouldn't open because Matt had braced his arm against it. She quickly retreated when he smiled at her. It wasn't a friendly smile. It was more a predatory leer.

"Matt, I want you to leave," she said uneasily.

He tucked the cigarettes into his pocket, leaned against the door and crossed his arms over his chest. "Why?"

"Because I want to be alone."

He regarded her through narrowed eyes. "You don't want to be alone, Doria. You just don't want to be with me. Why?"

"I can't believe you're so egotistical," she countered churlishly. When he didn't respond to her gibe, she said, "Okay, Matt, you asked for it. I nearly lost my job because of you. I've smeared my reputation because of you. I know that you think that's my just comeuppance for what I did to you fourteen years ago, and you're right. You've had your revenge, and the game's over."

"And what about Friday night?" he asked.

"What about it?"

His gaze drifted over her in a meaningful appraisal. "You know what I'm talking about. Now that you're no longer auditing my client, we can see each other openly."

"No," Doria stated firmly. "What happened Friday night was a mistake. We have nothing in common, Matt, and I never want to see you again."

"Tell me something, Doria. If I dressed in three-piece suits and ate at sushi bars, would you want to see me again?"

"No," Doria answered honestly.

"Then it's not my image that you're objecting to. It's me."

"No, it's me. I'm not the girl you knew, Matt. The day I walked out of the ghetto, she died, and I don't want to resurrect her."

"She didn't die, Doria. She's still inside you, and I'd bet my life savings that she's kicking and screaming to get out."

"Well, you'd be making a sucker bet," she retorted.

"No, I wouldn't, and I can prove it."

"How?" Doria asked suspiciously. "By trying to seduce me again?"

Matt released a dry laugh. "Nothing quite that blatant. All I have to do is walk over to your bookcase."

"My bookcase?" She glanced toward it quizzically. "What are you talking about?"

"Unicorns, griffins and dragons. They're the stuff of fairy tales."

"Don't be ridiculous," Doria muttered scornfully. "I don't believe in fairy tales and never have."

"Then why did you buy those figurines?"

"Because they're pretty, and I like pretty things."

"There are a lot of pretty things you could have collected, but you chose mythical beasts. They're whimsical, Doria, and whimsy doesn't fit in with the image you project. I think you bought them because it was the one safe outlet you could give that girl trapped inside."

"You don't know what you're talking about."

"Yes, Doria, I do," he corrected. "Several years ago I tried to pound myself into the nice little societal mode. Then, one morning I woke up feeling bruised and battered, and I realized it was because I was trying to pound a square peg into a round hole. For better or worse, we are the sum and substance of our lives. We can't walk away from it. What we can do is learn to accept who and what we are and use our experiences to our advantage."

"If I'd done that, I'd be rotting in jail right now," Doria drawled sarcastically.

"I doubt it. You were a survivor, Doria."

"I'm still a survivor, and I survive by conforming. You may be able to say to hell with convention, but you're a man living in a man's world. People will admire you because you're different. A woman doesn't have that luxury. She either plays by the rules or she stands in the unemployment line."

"I wish I could say you were wrong, but I know that in many cases you're right. And I'm not saying that you shouldn't live by the rules. I'm saying that you'll never be happy if you don't learn to mesh who you were with who you are."

"For your information, I was perfectly happy until you came charging into my life and turned it upside down," she informed him. "I knew who I was and where I was going. People admired and trusted me. Now, all that is gone and I have to start over."

She felt the tears rising again, but blinked against them bravely. "I deserve what happened to me, and I'll be the first to admit it. But I've paid my debt to you, Matt. Now it's time for you to say goodbye, climb onto your Harley-Davidson bike and roar off into the sunset."

"I can't do that, Doria."

"Why not?" she cried plaintively.

"Because I'm falling in love with you, and I think you feel the same way."

Doria felt the color draining from her face, and she shook her head in frantic denial. She couldn't handle her own love for Matt. There was no way she could handle him returning her feelings. "You're confusing love with lust."

"No, Doria. I know the difference. I just don't know if my feelings for you are strong enough to last a lifetime. Until I do, you aren't going to shake me."

Doria opened her mouth to argue further, but closed it when she noted the determined gleam in his eyes. Matt had his mind made up and nothing she said was going to change it. What she had to do was beat him at his own game.

She studied him as she pondered her strategy. Finally she said, "What you're saying is that you want to date me."

"That's right."

"All right, Matt. I'll date you if you give me your word that there will be no lovemaking."

"You've got to be joking!" he exclaimed in disbelief.

"I'm perfectly serious. You say your feelings for me are not based on lust, so prove it."

"Doria, after what happened Friday night, I don't know if I can keep a promise like that."

"Then you aren't falling in love with me. You're lusting after my body."

He scowled at her. "Dammit, Doria, that's emotional blackmail."

"That's my offer. Take it or leave it."

"Oh, I'll take it," he grumbled. "But I have a condition of my own. I'll keep my hands off you as long as you actively date me, and I'm not talking about one or two nights a week. I'm talking about seeing each other every night."

"I can't see you every night! I work, remember?"

"I won't deprive you of your sleep, but I want to see you every night. It's the only way I can guarantee that you're giving us a chance."

"Matt—" she began, only to have him interrupt.

"That's *my* offer, Doria. Take it or leave it."

This time, it was Doria who scowled. She wanted to tell him exactly what he could do with his offer, but she was convinced that the best way to get him out of her life was to agree. If they weren't making love, the more they dated, the faster that would happen.

"All right, Matt. I'll see you every night," she reluctantly acquiesced.

"Great. I'll be back at seven to take you to dinner. Wear a pair of jeans if you have them." With that, he left.

"What have I gotten myself into?" Doria muttered.

*A veritable mess,* her conscience answered tartly.

# 9

WHEN MATT ARRIVED promptly at seven, Doria decided that if nothing else, dating him would be interesting. Any other self-proclaimed suitor would bring her flowers or a bottle of wine. Matt showed up with a motorcycle helmet, a black leather jacket and a pair of matching gloves.

Doria accepted the gifts leerily. "Matt, you shouldn't have."

"You know me. Generous to the core," he responded with an easy grin.

"I hate to ask the obvious, but do you expect me to ride on your motorcycle?"

"Of course."

Doria shook her head. "Sorry, but I've never ridden a motorcycle and I don't intend to start now. They're too dangerous."

"Take my word for it. You're safer on the bike with me than you are in that tin can you drive."

"My car is not a tin can!" she exclaimed, affronted.

Matt chuckled. "I get it. Love me, love my car. Well, honey, that works both ways. Love me, love my bike."

"I wouldn't touch that line if you paid me to," she muttered disgruntledly.

"I'd be disappointed if you did." He held the jacket open for her.

"It's too hot for a leather jacket," she protested.

"You aren't wearing it for warmth," he explained. "If I should have to lay the bike down, leather is the best protection. It doesn't rip easily."

"What do you mean by 'lay the bike down'?" Doria inquired suspiciously.

"Use your imagination," Matt answered as he shook the jacket at her, a challenging gleam in his eye. "You aren't chicken, are you?"

Doria's common sense told her to refuse to go anywhere near his motorcycle, but it had been years since anyone had issued her a dare. She couldn't resist the challenge any more now than when she was a kid.

*So much for maturity,* she thought darkly as she slid into the jacket and pulled on the gloves, which might save her hands if she went sliding across pavement.

Matt eyed Doria with appreciation—denim and leather became her. It somehow softened her, made her more approachable. He wanted to sweep her into his arms, but confined himself to a long, slow look. He'd promised to keep his hands off her, and though he doubted it would be a promise he could keep, he had to make a token effort.

When his gaze reached her sneakered feet, he frowned. "Don't you have a pair of boots?"

"No, I don't have a pair of boots. I'm an IRS agent, not a moll."

"Well, you'll need a pair anyway. I'll buy them tomorrow," he stated, ignoring the fact that she was equating him with a gangster. He knew she was goading him to cover up her nervousness.

"You've already spent too much money on me," she objected. "This jacket alone had to have set you back a good penny."

"I don't sweat the pennies." He opened the door. "Come, my sweet. My trusty steed awaits us."

"I need to get my purse."

"All you need is your key, Doria." When she looked as if she'd object, he said, "I don't have saddlebags, so you'll have to hold on to a purse. Since you're not used to riding the bike, I'd prefer that you didn't have any distractions."

As a matter of principle, Doria wanted to argue with him, but reluctantly concluded that she'd hate ending up as a grease spot on the road over her purse. Grumbling, she retrieved her keys. After shooting Matt a defiant glance, she tucked her lipstick, a comb, some money and her driver's license into the zippered pocket of the jacket. In the event of disaster, she wanted the authorities to be able to identify her, and she never went anywhere without enough cab fare to get home.

"I'm ready," she finally told Matt.

He gestured for her to precede him. "After you."

When they reached the motorcycle, Matt helped her put on her helmet as he instructed, "There are only two rules you need to remember, Doria. The first is, keep your feet on the foot pegs even when I'm stopped. The second is, in the event of a crash, roll away from the bike so you don't get trapped beneath it."

"If you're trying to reassure me, Matt, you've failed miserably."

He tapped his finger against her nose before dropping her visor into place. "You worry too much."

While he put on his helmet, Doria eyed the motorcycle apprehensively. If she'd learned how to ride a bicycle, she might have had more faith in a two-wheel conveyance, but bicycles in the ghetto were almost as rare as a Rolls-Royce sedan. She was ready to admit her cowardice and beg Matt to take her car, but he swung his leg over the motorcycle and started the engine. Its roar effectively cut off any chance for talk and she'd never been good at charades. When he patted the seat behind him, she wavered. When he patted it more insistently, she climbed on.

He glanced from one side to the other, to make sure her feet were on the foot pegs. Then he yelled over his shoulder, "Hang on tight."

Doria took his order literally. She clung to him when he took off and began to mutter every prayer she'd ever learned. Unfortunately, she knew very few prayers, and she'd said all of them before they zoomed through the second stoplight. She hoped God gave credit for quality rather than quantity.

Matt came to a stop at the third traffic light and gave her hands a reassuring pat. For some reason, the gesture calmed Doria's racing heart. When they took off again, she found the courage to glance around her. With the wind buffeting her, she felt as if they were going a hundred miles an hour, but the scenery wasn't zipping by any faster than it did when she was in her car.

By the time Matt pulled onto the freeway ramp, Doria was beginning to enjoy the ride. And it did have some unique pluses, she concluded as Matt accelerated, causing his back to press firmly against her breasts and his bottom to nestle between her thighs. She could feel his muscles tensing and untensing as he maneuvered through traffic. She also became aware of the power vibrating beneath her. It was an exhilarating and strangely erotic sensation.

*Good heavens,* she thought in chagrin. *I'm getting turned on by a motorcycle!*

But it wasn't just the motorcycle. It was also Matt. This enforced closeness made her acutely conscious of every nuance of his body. She had accused him of lusting after her, but she was the one lusting now. She wanted to slide her hands inside his jacket and stroke his chest. She wanted to touch his groin to ascertain whether he was as affected by her as she was by him. The thought was so tempting that she tightened her hold around his waist to keep from acting on it. Touching him that intimately at fifty-five miles an hour was definitely a traffic hazard.

When Matt finally exited the freeway and entered a large warehouse district, Doria was puzzled. They were supposed to be going to dinner, so why was he stopping here?

He drove through a maze of streets that were well lit but seemed threatening because of the dark, looming shadows of warehouses. Finally, he pulled to a stop in front of a small, run-down building. There was a neon sign in the window that read: ood. Doria assumed it was supposed to read food and that the *F* had burned out, though considering the look of the place, it wasn't a certainty. Since Matt had turned off the engine, she dismounted and removed her helmet.

"Hope you're hungry," Matt said as he stood, whipped off his helmet and hung it on one of the handlebars. He took hers and hung it on the other one. "Milly's food is not only good, but is served in man-size portions."

"Well, I hope you're hungry enough for one and a half men," Doria responded as she gazed up at him. He looked sexier than ever with his hair tousled and his cheeks ruddy from the wind. "I gain weight from just smelling food. I can't afford to eat man-size portions."

Matt's gaze skimmed over her, lingering at her full breasts and her rounded hips. She wasn't model slender, but she was a far cry from fat. He became aroused at the remembrance of how soft she'd felt when they'd made love. She wasn't hard angles and jutting planes, but satiny, pliable curves.

"I've always had a fondness for Rubenesque women," he said gruffly as he took her hand and led her toward the restaurant. If he didn't get her into a crowd, he'd probably attack her right in the parking lot.

When they walked into the restaurant, she gaped in disbelief. Fishnets and Chinese lanterns cluttered the ceiling. The back wall was a black-and-white mural of eyes in every size and shape. The wall on the right was a red-and-white mural of mouths, and the wall on the left was a blue-and-white mural of gigantic, bulbous noses.

She was still trying to take it all in when a section of the eye-covered wall flew open, revealing the kitchen. A behemoth of a man exited. He had to be seven feet tall if he was an inch, and she was sure that he weighed at least four hundred pounds. He was bald, but what he lacked in hair on his head, he made up for by a bushy black beard wild enough to provide a habitat for a family of mice. He plopped bowls the size of soup tureens in front of two men at the back table. Then he wiped his hands on a soiled white apron and glanced toward her and Matt.

Doria jumped when he let out a deafening bellow and began to charge toward them, shaking the building with the force of an earthquake. If Matt hadn't been holding her hand, she would have run for her life. When the man reached them, he grabbed Matt in a bear hug that Doria was sure would break his back.

"Matt! Where the hell have you been?" the brute asked.

"Working, Milly," Matt answered with a laugh as he stepped back. "Doria, this is Millard Turner. Milly, Doria Sinclair."

"I'm glad to meet you, Mr. Turner," Doria murmured.

"Call me Milly," he said, extending a hand the size of a small ham.

Doria cautiously accepted it. "Only if you call me Doria."

His handshake was firm but gentle. "Doria, it is." He glanced toward Matt, mischief in his eyes. "How did an SOB like you hook up with a nice girl like this?"

"SOB?" Matt repeated, outraged though he was grinning widely. "Is that any way to talk about a friend?"

"Friends don't stay away for months on end," Milly told him, also feigning outrage. "So, what have you been up to?"

"Working my tail off," Matt replied. "From the reports you've sent me, you've been working pretty hard yourself."

Milly shrugged. "What can I say? Chef's Surprise is the hit of the warehouse district. But you didn't come here to talk business. Let's get you seated."

A moment later, they were settled at a table and Milly had hurried back to the kitchen.

When he was gone, Doria asked, "Is Milly one of your clients?"

"No. I'm his business partner."

"You own part of this place?" Doria gasped. "Why?"

"I like Milly's cooking, and this place is a gold mine."

"A gold mine?" Doria repeated skeptically.

Matt nodded. "There are more than a hundred-and-fifty warehouses around here. The workers have to eat somewhere. Chef's Surprise not only serves good food, but it's plentiful and the price is reasonable."

"You mean prices," Doria noted.

"I mean price. There's only one item on the menu, and it's whatever Milly has concocted for the day," he explained.

"I get it. It's the chef's surprise."

He grinned. "You're quick."

"How did you hook up with Milly?" she asked next.

"That's a long and boring story," Matt answered too nonchalantly.

Doria eyed him shrewdly. "That means it's probably a short and dangerous story. I'd like to hear it."

"I'd rather not talk about it," Matt grumbled.

"Fine. I'll ask Milly what happened."

"The hell you will," he countered, scowling.

By now, Doria's curiosity was reaching a fever pitch. If Matt was so opposed to telling the story, then it had to be hot stuff.

"Come on, Matt," she urged, using her most coaxing tone. "You can tell me about it."

"Dammit, Doria, it's too embarrassing, so let's drop the subject, okay?"

"Not okay. If you won't tell me, I'll ask Milly what happened."

Matt rolled his eyes heavenward as if seeking divine guidance. Finally he released a sigh of resignation and said, "I was mugged and Milly helped me out."

"What's embarrassing about that?" Doria questioned in confusion.

Matt blushed crimson. "They stole my clothes."

"They stole your clothes?" When Matt nodded, she asked, "All of them?" When he nodded again, she burst into roaring laughter.

"There's nothing funny about being stranded in an alley, buck naked," Matt stated crossly. "It was raining and it was cold. If Milly hadn't come along, I might have died from hypothermia."

Doria tried to stifle her laughter. When she managed to get herself down to intermittent giggles, she said, "You're right, Matt. It isn't funny."

"So why are you still giggling?"

"Because it isn't the kind of thing I'd expect to happen to you."

"Well, it wasn't something I expected to happen to me, either, but it did. Now, let's talk about something else."

"Okay. What do you want to talk about?"

"How about your most embarrassing moment?"

"Sorry, but I don't have any embarrassing moments that would come close to matching yours."

"Come on, Doria. Everyone has embarrassing moments."

"That's true, but mine are very mundane. I lead a quiet life, Matt."

"Don't you ever get the urge to break loose and do something outrageous?"

"Sure, but I ignore it. As you recall, that kind of impetuosity got me into a lot of trouble as a kid."

"Just because you've grown up doesn't mean you can't have fun."

"I have fun."

"What kind of fun?" Matt asked.

"Oh, you know, the regular kind of stuff. I go out to dinner. See a movie. Go to a play."

Matt started to tell her that those activities were conventional entertainment and not the type of fun he was referring to. Thankfully, Milly showed up with their food before he could utter the words. Matt had a feeling he'd make better inroads with her if he showed her what he was talking about instead of lecturing her on the subject.

"This looks wonderful!" Doria told Milly as she eyed the food in her bowl. It looked like a cross between seafood chowder and some type of stew. "What's in it?"

"Fish, fish and more fish. The rest of the ingredients are a secret," Milly answered, beaming at her compliment.

"In other words, he's forgotten what he's put in it," Matt teased.

"You'd better hope I haven't," Milly countered with a grin. "This is one of my bestsellers. And speaking of bestsellers, I'd better take care of the rest of my customers. Enjoy."

"I've never tasted anything so delicious," Doria stated after taking a bite. "Milly's wasting his talents here. He should open a decent restaurant."

"This *is* a decent restaurant, Doria," Matt chided quietly.

Doria blushed. "I know that, Matt. I just meant—"

"I know what you meant," he interrupted, softening his words with an understanding smile. "But Milly's happy here. He can cook what he wants when he wants, and his customers are always satisfied."

"He could do the same at a more upscale restaurant," Doria argued.

Matt shook his head. "In a more upscale restaurant people wouldn't be coming in to eat, they'd be coming in to dine. He'd have to come up with a set menu, and he wouldn't be able to mingle with his customers. They'd take one look at him and run."

"That's a cruel thing to say, Matt."

"Is it? Tell me the truth, Doria. What was your reaction when you first saw Milly?"

"All right, you have a point," Doria conceded. "But when people got to know him, they wouldn't feel that way."

"And how many people are going to hang around long enough to get to know him? One out of every five? One out of every ten? At that rate, he'd go out of business in a week."

"You've just made me feel an inch tall," Doria murmured as she stirred her food despondently.

Matt reached across the table and caught her hand, giving it a comforting squeeze. "I didn't mean to do that. I was only trying to make you see that you don't tamper with success in order to create a better image, particularly when that image is going to make a person unhappy."

Matt wasn't just talking about Milly—he was also referring to her. The worst part was, she basically agreed with him. At least, when it came to Milly. Her own circumstances were different. She hadn't created a better image from success. She'd become successful because of the image she'd created. She couldn't explain that to him, however, because then she'd have to tell him about all her lies. The one thing Matt had never been able to tolerate was a liar.

*Which is exactly why you should tell him. It would get him out of your life for good.*

But as she looked into his eyes and saw the remorse he felt for making her feel bad, she knew that she didn't want Matt out of her life. She was in love with him, and he claimed he was falling in love with her. With a feeling of déjà vu, she realized that if she'd told him everything from the beginning, they might have had a chance. Now, it was too late. She felt the sting of tears.

"Doria, I'm sorry," Matt murmured when he saw her eyes glisten with tears. "I didn't mean to hurt your feelings."

"You didn't," she said softly, tremulously. "It's just that . . ."

"It's just that what?" he prompted.

She shook her head. "I'm confused about so many things right now, but there is one thing I'm not confused about."

"And what's that?"

"I want to make love with you. Do you think we could go home?"

Matt blinked, certain he'd misunderstood her, but her expression assured him he hadn't.

"You said no lovemaking," he reminded.

"It's a woman's prerogative to change her mind."

"Then let's get the hell out of here." He shot to his feet, grabbed her hand, pulled her out of her chair and hurried her toward the door.

When they exited, however, he didn't head for his motorcycle. He led her around the corner of the building. There, he pushed her up against the wall and braced a hand on either side of her head.

"Doria, before we take another step, I need to know if you have any doubts. I don't want to make love to you tonight, only to have you filled with regret in the morning."

It was dark, but there was enough illumination from the streetlight for Doria to read Matt's expression. It was tight-lipped and tense, but the hot glow in his eyes confirmed that he wanted her as badly as she wanted him.

Did she have doubts? Of course, but they were not about making love with him. They were centered on how she was going to survive when Matt learned about her lies and walked away from her. And if he became her lover, he would eventually learn about them.

If she admitted having doubts, Matt would keep his distance. When he finally walked away, it wouldn't hurt as badly. She also wouldn't have the memories of him to relive in the long lonely years that stretched ahead.

"The only doubt I have," she murmured huskily, "is that I don't know if I can last long enough to make it back to my apartment. Isn't your place closer?"

"Oh, Doria," Matt breathed as he bent his elbows and let his body press against hers. His lips sought hers, and he groaned when she parted them in welcome. He plunged his tongue into her mouth, eager to reacquaint himself with her taste. She was so sweet and soft and hot.

"My place is closer," he rasped as he jerked away from the kiss. "But I'll have to drag you out of bed before dawn to get you home in time to dress for work."

Matt's kiss had been so devastating that Doria had to swallow hard to find her voice. Even then, it was nothing more than a hoarse whisper as she said, "I'm on vacation this week."

"Then, my place it is."

DORIA CAME TO the conclusion that riding a motorcycle was a rousing form of foreplay. The bike's power made her feel reckless. The wind whipping at her made her feel free. The press of Matt's body against hers made her hungry for love.

When Matt pulled off the freeway and stopped at a traffic light, she daringly slid her hand to his groin, thrilled to discover that he was as ready for her as she was for him. His entire body went rigid at her touch, but when she started to pull her hand away, he held it in place.

Matt was shaking by the time he pulled into his drive. Doria's hand still held him intimately, and his penis was swollen to the point where he was sure it would burst out of its skin. He turned off the engine and gulped in several breaths of air, telling himself that he couldn't throw her down on the grass and take her.

Doria sensed that Matt was on the brink of losing his control, and it filled her with a sense of feminine power. She was tempted to push him to the limit, but she didn't want to dominate Matt. She wanted to make love with him as an equal.

She climbed off the motorcycle and removed her helmet. Then she stood waiting for him to join her, so attuned to him that she could feel the struggle going on inside him. When he heaved in a deep breath and his shoulders relaxed, she knew he'd finally won the battle.

"You're damn bold, honey," he said gruffly as he stood beside her and removed his helmet.

"Are you complaining?" she asked as she gazed up at him.

He shook his head. "I like a bold woman."

"Then why don't we go inside so I can show you just how bold I am?"

Matt shuddered at her provocative words and extended his hand to her. When she took it, he pulled her up against him. He searched her eyes. What he found was a need that matched his own.

"I want to make love to you slow and easy," he told her hoarsely.

"I'm in the mood for fast and hard," Doria murmured huskily as she slid her hand inside his jacket and kneaded her fingernails against his T-shirt.

"Oh, damn," he rasped.

He may have initiated the kiss, but Doria took control. She traced his mouth with her tongue until she'd memorized its shape and texture. Then she went deeper, tasting and teasing and exploring.

He released a guttural groan and swung her up into his arms, moving toward the house with a purposeful stride. When they entered, the hall light was on, and he headed for the stairs.

"You'd better put me down. I'm too heavy for you to carry me upstairs," Doria murmured.

Matt released a low, dry laugh. "Honey, right now I feel as strong as Atlas, and you aren't that heavy."

"Matt—"

"Hush," he whispered as he caught her lips in a searing kiss. By the time he let her come up for air, they were in his bedroom.

He dropped her to the bed and came over her. The next few minutes were filled with moans and sighs as they undressed each other with frantic urgency.

"Fast and hard!" Doria demanded breathlessly as she kicked off her jeans and panties and reached for Matt.

"Fast and hard," he agreed. "You're so hot!"

"That's because I'm burning up for you!" She thrust her hips upward, drawing the tip of his shaft inside her.

With a groan, Matt flexed his hips and drove the remainder of the way into her. Doria whimpered his name, but her tone assured him that she wasn't in pain. He withdrew and entered her again. With an endearing curse, he rolled, pulling her over him.

"Ride me, honey," he urged as he slid his hands up the smooth length of her back. He tangled his fingers in her hair and eased her head back. His lips found hers, and he kissed her with all the hunger inside him.

Doria shuddered, though she didn't know if it was from the ardency of his kiss or his coarse request that she ride him. She rotated her hips against his and sighed into his mouth at the stimulating friction.

He released her from the kiss and eased her upward until she was sitting astride him. Grasping her waist, he lifted her and then brought her down to meet him. Doria needed no further instructions and settled her hands on his shoulders as she set a fast-faced rhythm. She gasped when Matt slid his hand between them and touched her. His fingers stroked her until she was writhing against his hand. She was so close to climax that she ached, but she instinctively fought release.

"Let it go, honey. Don't fight it," Matt rasped.

"I . . . can't . . . let . . . go," she stammered raggedly.

"Sure, you can." He continued stroking her sensitive nub as he brought his free hand up to her breasts and plucked at one swollen nipple and then the other.

"Matt!" she moaned.

"I can't last much longer," he announced tersely as he continued his torment. "Let it go, honey. I want you to come with me."

"Yes. I want— Oh!" she cried in relief as the wave hit.

"Oh, yes!" Matt shouted as he gripped her hips and surged upward until he was buried so deep inside her he could feel the mouth of her womb. He let himself go.

He was still shuddering from his release when Doria collapsed on his chest. He ran his hands down her back, over the soft globes of her buttocks, down her thighs, and then reversed the journey. When he reached her neck, he massaged it lightly.

Doria closed her eyes, enjoying Matt's caresses. She knew she should be exhausted, but she'd never felt more alert or alive. She could lie with him like this forever, but she was sure he was growing tired of supporting her weight.

She began to shift off him, but he held her in place. "Where are you going?"

"I'm just getting off you. You must be crushed."

"I'm fine," he said, settling her back into place.

"But, Matt—"

"Don't argue with me, honey. I'm feeling too mellow."

She propped her forearms on his chest and looked at his face. The only illumination in the room was a shaft of moonlight, so she couldn't see his expression.

"What are you thinking?" he asked with amused tolerance.

*That I'm madly in love with you and will be until the day I die,* she answered inwardly. Aloud, she said, "Why is this happening between us, Matt?"

"I don't know."

"Doesn't it worry you?"

"Why should it worry me?"

"Because you hated me for so long, and I can't believe that you can dismiss those feelings so easily."

"Whoa. We're getting into a heavy-duty subject here." He shifted them until he could reach the lamp. He switched it on. They both blinked blindly for a moment.

When their eyes grew accustomed to the light, he caught her chin between his thumb and forefinger and said, "I never hated you, Doria."

"Of course, you did. I deprived you of your last days with your father."

"I deprived myself of the last days with my father," Matt countered grimly. "I knew you'd stolen that car, but I still climbed into it."

"But if I hadn't let you take the fall, you'd have been with your father."

Matt shook his head. "I've thought a lot about this the last few weeks, and I now realize that if I hadn't gotten into trouble then, I would have gotten into trouble later. My father raised me to know the difference between right and wrong, and I chose wrong because I wanted to punish him."

Doria frowned in bewilderment. "That doesn't make sense, Matt. You loved your father."

"Yes," he stated with a heavy sigh. "I also hated him for his illness. If he hadn't been sick, we wouldn't have been stuck in the ghetto. I know that sounds warped, but I was a kid. Unfortunately, the adolescent brain functions on emotion rather than logic. By the time I got everything straightened out in my head, he was gone. I couldn't make amends with him, so I blamed you. It was easier to hate you than it was to face my own guilt."

"I'm still to blame for what happened, Matt. Whenever you look at me, you have to relive that agony."

"There's only one thing I feel when I look at you," Matt drawled as he rolled, pulling her beneath him.

"And what's that?" Doria asked breathlessly, though the question was moot. His answer was pressed firmly against her abdomen.

"Horny as hell," he answered with a wolfish grin. "We did it your way. Fast and hard. Now we're going to do it my way. Slow and easy."

"Mmm," she hummed as she ran her hand over his chest and tangled her fingers in the mat of dark hair. "Don't you think we should take a shower first?"

"Yeah," he muttered as he stared down at her breasts. They were as pale as alabaster, with dainty, rose-tipped peaks. "We've made love twice, but I still don't know you intimately. I'll wash you, and you can wash me. Then we'll know each other's bodies as well as we know our own."

By the time they were halfway through their shower, Doria decided that Matt knew her body better than she ever could. But that was okay. She also knew his just as intimately.

When they stepped out of the shower, Matt didn't bother with towels. He carried her to the bed, where they made slow, easy love. As her lips and hands explored him, he told her what he liked with groans and lusty requests. When he returned the favor, Doria was too far gone to realize that she was talking to him in the same manner.

Matt, however, was well aware of her vernacular. Gone was the prim and proper, designer-label Barbie doll. In her place was an earthy woman that he found enthralling. When she wrapped her arms around his neck and brought him down for a kiss, he settled between her thighs. Doria opened to him eagerly, and "slow and easy" suddenly became "fast and hard."

# 10

WHEN MATT AWOKE, he'd never felt more contented in his life. Doria was cuddled against him with her head on his shoulder. He rested his cheek against her hair and listened to her gentle breathing.

If he'd had any doubts that he was in love with her, last night had alleviated them. When they'd made love, she'd shed her pretenses and let the real woman surface. She'd been earthy without being crude, brazen without being crass. In another woman he might have written off her actions as experienced, but he knew Doria's response hadn't come from experience. She wasn't a physical virgin, yet there had been an underlying shyness and vulnerability in her lovemaking that had convinced him she was an emotional one. Or at least she had been until last night, when she'd given herself to him freely and completely.

His heart expanded and his body stirred at that revelation. He was in love, and he let his hand glide down her body. It was the only way he could convince himself she wasn't a dream.

"Matt? What time is it?" Doria murmured sleepily.

He pressed a kiss against her hair. "Early. Go back to sleep."

"I can't believe it," she grumbled as she levered herself up on an elbow. "You even give orders at dawn."

When she started to shift away from him, he held her in place. "I guess I'm a born leader."

"What you are is bossy."

He grinned. "As I recall, you were pretty bossy yourself, last night."

"Yes, well . . ." Doria murmured, ducking her head as color flooded her cheeks.

Matt caught her chin and raised it, forcing her to look at him. "There's nothing to be embarrassed about, Doria."

"I'm not embarrassed. I'm perplexed. Last night... Well, it's never been like that before."

Matt reached up to smooth her tangled curls. "Well, believe it or not, I feel the same way. No woman has ever gotten under my skin the way you have. You enchant me and infuriate me. Whenever I'm with you, I feel as if I've climbed on one of those wild roller-coaster rides at Disneyland."

"I know exactly what you mean," Doria said as she touched his whiskered jaw. The feel of it was so manly, so virile. She rubbed her palm against it. "I've always heard that sex is supposed to be like this, but I never believed it until now."

"We don't have sex, honey," Matt corrected as he rolled, trapping her beneath him. Then he dropped a chaste kiss to her lips. It made him ravenous for more. "We make love. And believe me, there's a big difference."

"Oh, yeah? How about showing me?"

"Gladly," he rasped as he set about doing just that.

AS SHE DID EVERY MONTH, Doria stood in Dr. Gregory's office and stared out the window at the small duck pond on the nursing-home grounds. Her eyes weren't on the ducks, however. They were searching the faces of the men sitting beneath the shade trees, looking for her father.

"Good afternoon, Doria," Dr. Gregory said as she entered her office. "I was surprised to learn you were here on a weekday."

"Good afternoon, Dr. Gregory," Doria returned to the tall rawboned woman whose hair was white but whose face was as unlined as a newborn babe's. "I'm on vacation this week, so I came early."

Dr. Gregory nodded as she poured herself a cup of coffee and joined Doria at the window. They were quiet for several minutes before the woman said, "He still refuses to see you. I'm sorry."

"Yes," Doria said. "It's so nice out. I thought he might be at the pond."

"He normally would be, but today he refused to go outside."

"It's as if he knows when I'm coming, isn't it?"

"Why do you keep coming, Doria? Why do you put yourself through this?"

"He's my father," Doria answered simply.

"He's also a very emotionally disturbed man."

"He's had a massive stroke."

"He was disturbed before the stroke, Doria," the doctor chided gently.

"He was fine until my mother died. It did something to him," Doria automatically defended.

"Other people lose their spouses, and they don't abuse their children."

"We've been through this before, Dr. Gregory," Doria stated in vexation.

"And as long as you insist on coming here, I'm going to insist on going through it again," Dr. Gregory responded. "I know you love your father, but there is such a thing as fighting a losing battle. For your own emotional well-being, you have to stop setting yourself up for his rejection."

"And I keep telling you that no matter how many times he rejects me, at least he knows I've been here. That has to be worth something."

"Have you ever stopped to think that maybe it makes him feel worse? If you won't give yourself some peace, then give him some."

"Are you saying that my visits harm him?" Doria asked anxiously.

"They don't help him," the doctor answered. "He's very fragile, both physically and emotionally. He becomes extremely agitated whenever he learns you're here. If he becomes too overwrought, he could have another stroke. For both your sakes, stay away, Doria. If he changes his mind and wants to see you, I'll call."

Doria returned her attention to the duck pond, her chest aching with so much pain she could barely breathe. She knew her father would never change his mind. He hated her, and today the finality of that sank in.

MATT KNEW THERE WAS something wrong with Doria the moment he arrived at her apartment. Dinner was over, however, before he was able to put his finger on it. She was too bright and cheerful. In fact, now that he'd pinpointed the problem, he realized she was almost frenzied.

"So, what did you do today?" he asked as he helped her load the dishwasher.

"Some laundry and some shopping. I spent most of the day sitting around being lazy."

"So what happened to upset you?"

Doria nearly dropped the plate she was rinsing. She should have realized that Matt would see through her cheerful facade. Why hadn't she cancelled dinner after her visit to the nursing home? Because tonight of all nights, she couldn't bear to be alone.

"Nothing happened," she lied glibly. "Why would you think I'm upset?"

"Well, for one thing, you're cramming those forks into the garbage disposal."

"Oh, damn!" She held the forks under the light to examine them. "I just bought this flatware, and now I've probably scratched it."

"They're just forks," Matt said impatiently as he took them from her hand and dropped them into the dishwasher. "They can be replaced."

Doria's temper flared, though she knew she wasn't angry with Matt. She was angry at her father, and Matt just happened to be the handy outlet.

"Maybe they can be replaced," she stated disdainfully, "but they're expensive. You might be able to throw your money away, but . . ."

She was using that damn haughty tone again, and Matt's temper erupted. He grabbed her arms and gave her a small shake. "Dammit, Doria, we aren't talking about the cost of forks or how I spend my money. We're talking about you, so stop playing games with me. You're upset. I want to know why."

"I am *not* upset!" she declared angrily. "Or at least I wasn't until you started manhandling me."

"I am not manhandling you," he stated in a clipped tone. He removed his hands from her arms and stuffed them into his pockets while wrestling his temper back under control. "I'm also not going to let you start a fight to get me off the subject. I asked you a simple question. Now, I'd like a simple answer."

"I gave you a simple answer. It appears, however, that it isn't the one you want to hear."

"What I want to hear is the truth, Doria."

"Are you calling me a liar?"

"Would I be accurate if I was?"

Doria closed the door of the dishwasher before saying, "I think you'd better leave, Matt."

"I'm not going anywhere," he responded as he leaned a hip against the counter and crossed his arms over his chest. "I'm going to stand right here until you tell me who or what upset you."

"All right, have it your way," Doria snapped as she perched her hands on her hips and glared at him. "You want to know what upset me? When I went to the grocery store today, I found out that lettuce has gone up ten cents a pound and tomatoes have gone up twenty cents a pound. If that wasn't bad enough, chicken is so expensive it should be gold plated. Then I came home with my Fort Knox groceries and fixed supper for my lover. Did I get a polite, 'This is really good, Doria. Thank you.' for my effort? No. You give me the third degree and call me a liar!"

"I never called you a liar."

"You implied that I was one."

"Are you?"

"Ooh! I'm getting out of here before I strangle you."

She headed for the living room and Matt followed her, saying, "You didn't answer my question."

"I won't dignify it with an answer."

"Fine. You can tell me what's wrong instead."

"Nothing's wrong!" she yelled as she threw herself down onto the sofa and grabbed a light-blue throw pillow, hugging it to her stomach. She couldn't believe it when Matt snatched the cushion away from her and threw it across the room.

"Just what do you think you're doing?" she demanded as she shot to her feet.

"Getting rid of your defenses. You're not going to hide from this discussion. What happened today?"

"Nothing!"

"You know, Doria, right now is one of those times when I don't know whether to kiss you or shake you. What I do know is that you're hurting. Let me help."

"If you really want to help, Matt, then drop this. Please."

Matt searched her face. She was so pale, she looked ghostly. Her eyes were large, shimmering blue moons. She was biting her lower lip, and he suspected it was because it was trembling. Instinct told him to handle her with kid gloves and he decided to follow his instincts.

He opened his arms and said, "Come here, honey, and let me hold you."

It wasn't Matt's words as much as the gentle way in which he delivered them that destroyed Doria's fragile control. With a sob, she fell into his arms. When they wrapped around her tightly, she burst into a flood of tears.

Matt had never felt more helpless. He'd handled crying women before, but Doria wasn't just crying. She was hysterical. When she began to shake from the intensity of her sobs, he swung her up into his arms and sat on the sofa, cradling her on his lap. He stroked her back and her hair. He murmured soothing platitudes in her ear. He didn't know if his actions were helping her, but he felt better.

He had no idea how much time had passed when her tears began to lessen. It could have been minutes or hours. It had felt like days.

"I'm sorry," Doria finally whispered.

"Oh, honey, you don't have anything to be sorry about," Matt murmured as he pressed his cheek to her hair. "Sometimes a person needs to indulge in a good cry to make them feel better."

"Do you ever indulge in a good cry?" she asked.

"No. When I'm feeling blue, I go out and beat up muggers."

Doria released a watery giggle. "I can see you doing exactly that."

"Yeah, well, what can I say?" When she didn't respond, he said, "Since you feel better, how about telling me why you're so upset."

Doria instinctively balked at the suggestion. "I can't."

"Can't or won't?" he asked as he shifted her on his arm so he could see her face. He brushed her tear-soaked hair away from her cheek.

"Can't," she answered. "I lied to you, Matt."

"If you lied to me, I'm sure you had a good reason. Why don't you tell me about it?" he encouraged.

Again, she balked, but as she stared up into his eyes, which were full of so much warmth and caring, she found herself wanting to tell him the whole sordid story. She needed to unload the burden. It had become too heavy for her to carry alone.

She shifted her head back to his chest. It would be easier to talk if she didn't have to look at him. She could also listen to the beating of his heart, which she found inordinately comforting.

"I told you my father is dead, but he isn't. He had a massive stroke a year ago and is in a nursing home a few miles from here."

"I see," Matt said, forcing himself to remain relaxed. He wasn't upset by Doria's revelation. He was fighting against all the old memories of what she'd looked like following one of her father's beatings. His stomach began to burn. "What's his prognosis?"

"He's a paraplegic and there's no hope for him to get better. If he'd had medical attention right after the stroke, maybe things would be different, but . . ."

She shivered and Matt cuddled her closer. "But what, honey?"

"He lay in bed for several days before the landlord found him, and it's my fault. I should have arranged for someone to check on him, but I was angry with him. When I first started working I sent him money. It wasn't a fortune, but it was enough to get him out of that damn hovel. He sent it back."

"Then you have nothing to feel guilty about, Doria. He made the choice not to accept your help."

"I still should have arranged for someone to check on him. I could have called one of the missions. I could have sent them the money, and they could have taken him food and kept an eye on him. Why didn't I do that, Matt? Why did I sit around feeling sorry for myself instead of helping him?"

"Honey, you are not your father's keeper. He's a grown man. He's responsible for his own life."

"He hates me, Matt. I go to the nursing home and he refuses to see me. Today, his doctor told me not to come back. She says just knowing I'm there upsets him to the point that he could have another stroke."

Matt's heart lurched at the pain in her voice. If he could have held her any closer, he would have, but she was already pressed as tightly to him as possible. "Why won't he see you, Doria?"

"Because of my mother. My father adored her. They were juniors in high school when they fell in love, and then my mother got pregnant with me. My father had to drop out of school to get a job. After I was born, he was supposed to finish school, but my mother developed diabetes during the pregnancy and they never did get it under control."

She paused for several minutes before continuing, "The medical bills kept piling up, and my father couldn't keep up with them. Finally, he quit his job so we could go on welfare. When my mother's kidneys failed, there was nothing he could do. He was uneducated and unskilled, and there was no way he could earn the money for the dialysis she needed. When she died, he told me that if I hadn't been born, she wouldn't have gotten sick."

"That's ridiculous!" Matt exclaimed, horrified that any parent would dump that kind of guilt on a child's head.

"No. It's a fact. My mother gave birth to me, and because she did, she died. Every time my father looked at me, I was a reminder of what he'd lost."

"And that's why he abused you," Matt said in sudden understanding.

"He couldn't help it, Matt. He adored my mother, and I killed her."

Matt ached for her, but he didn't know what to say. She was an intelligent, educated woman. If anyone else had made the statement she'd just made, he was sure she'd have recognized the absurdity of their words. But she was talking about herself. She couldn't be objective.

"Doria, have you ever thought about counseling?" he asked.

She glanced up at him in puzzlement. "For what?"

"For your feelings about everything that's happened to you."

"I know what my feelings are. I don't need any counselor to explain them."

"Honey, I know you had psychology courses in school. You're a textbook case of child abuse. In order to live your life to its fullest potential, you need to come to grips with your past. The best way to do that is to get some professional help."

"No!" Doria sprang to her feet and began to pace. "Counseling is for people who can't cope. I cope perfectly. I hold down a job. I handle my bills. I'm not an alcoholic and I don't take drugs. I don't have fits of depression or exhibit any other form of psychotic behavior. I'm a respectable member of society."

Matt eyed her narrowly. "In other words, respectable members of society don't seek counseling."

"Of course, they do," she muttered. "But they do it because they're having difficulty coping. I don't have that problem."

Matt wanted to point out that the crying jag she'd just had was not typical of a person who was in control. He refrained, recognizing it would only anger her. It would also be cruel. Eventually, he'd get her into counseling. It would just take time and patience to help her see that she needed it. In the meantime, he'd devote himself to loving her as she should be loved—completely and unreservedly.

"Well, my respectable member of society," he drawled sexily, "do you think you could come over here and give this disreputable member of society a kiss?"

"You don't want to kiss me," Doria mumbled as she swiped at her tearstained cheeks. "I look like hell."

"You look a bit worse for wear," Matt acknowledged. "But you don't look like hell. Even if you did, I'd still want to kiss you, so come here."

His voice had been coaxing, but it was his eyes that drew Doria to him. They were dark green pools of hungry sensuality, convincing her that he wasn't lying. That he wanted to kiss her—and more. She wanted his kiss, but it was the "more" that she yearned for. She needed to be held and touched and loved.

When she sank into Matt's arms, he tumbled her onto the sofa. Then he went about fulfilling every one of those needs. When he was finished, he carried her to bed and set about doing it all again.

By the time Doria fell asleep, cradled securely in his arms, she knew that the pain of her father's rejection would always be overshadowed by the euphoria she'd just experienced in Matt's arms.

# 11

As Matt watched Doria dress for work, he experienced an odd mingling of concern and fear. Though they hadn't discussed it, he knew she was tense about returning to the office. He wanted to reassure her, to tell her that she had nothing to worry about. Unfortunately, that wasn't true.

Her replacement, Andy Cross, was an affable, talkative man. It had been easy to discover that her coworkers' speculations regarding her removal from the audit ranged from incompetency to taking a bribe. Ironically, no one seemed to have considered the truth.

All week, Matt had been torn about telling her what he'd learned. The honorable side of his nature insisted that he should alert her to what she would face. He feared, however, the consequences of such an act. If he told her, she'd be reminded that he was the cause of her fall from grace. All the tenuous ground he'd gained with her might be wiped out.

"I like you better in jeans, even if they do have those fancy designer labels on the back pocket," he drawled as she stepped into her skirt.

Doria glanced up in surprise. She'd been so busy trying to garner her courage to face the day ahead that she'd forgotten Matt. He'd propped the pillows behind his back and slung the sheet over his hips, but she seemed to have developed X-ray vision. A perfect image of him boldly naked arose in her mind. Immediately on its heels came images of elephants and giraffes. An unexpected giggle escaped her.

Matt eyed her in wary question. "What's so funny?"

"Elephants and giraffes," Doria answered teasingly.

His brows drew together in a puzzled frown. "Elephants and giraffes?"

She nodded as she lowered her gaze to his lap. "Halliford gave you a couple of interesting zoological jockstraps. I wondered if you'd do them justice, and now that I know..."

"You find it laughable?" Matt exclaimed in disbelief. "There's nothing laughable about a man's . . . manhood!"

"Is *that* what it's called these days?" Doria asked, her eyes sparkling with devilish mirth.

His scowl deepened as he sat up stiffly. "By damn, woman, I have half a notion to drag you into bed and make you eat your words!"

"I'd rather you modeled your jockstraps so I can see just how well you fill them out," she purred sexily.

He smiled as his gaze strayed to her breasts and then down to her hips. "Tell you what. We'll get some of Halliford's interesting merchandise for you, and we'll model for each other."

Doria's cheeks reddened. "I think I'd like that."

With a growl, Matt tossed back the sheet and bounded out of bed. When he reached her, he raised her face to his.

"It's going to be tough today, honey. Be strong and hold your head high. They can only hurt you if you let them."

The worried concern reflected in his eyes and bracketing his mouth touched Doria deeply. "I won't let them hurt me."

"Good girl," he said on a sigh of relief as he noted the determination in her eyes. "God, you are so sexy that it's mind-blowing."

"Your mind seems to have slipped down a few feet," Doria quipped as she skimmed her hand over his stomach and touched his erection. "If I wasn't running late, I'd tumble you to the bed and have my way with you."

"You can do that tonight." Matt dropped a light kiss to her lips. He wanted to smear her lipstick, but he restrained himself, concluding that he rather liked Doria's prim-and-proper persona. It meant that no one would ever suspect the passion that rested beneath the surface. That was a secret he intended to keep to himself.

When Matt drew away from the kiss, Doria rested her head against his chest and listened to the strong beat of his heart. Suddenly, all the fear she'd been experiencing dissipated. She might be the focus of the office gossip-mill; but as Matt had said, they couldn't hurt her unless she let them.

"Are you okay?" Matt asked gruffly.

Doria tilted her head back and smiled flirtatiously. "Nothing's wrong that you can't fix tonight."

"You're damn right," he mumbled as he caught her face in his hands. "And don't you forget it."

WHEN DORIA RANG Matt's doorbell, she recognized that the anticipation she felt was dangerous. She and Matt had been seeing each other officially for two weeks. By now, the chemistry between them should have been waning, but it was growing stronger. Logically, she knew that their relationship would eventually have to end. Emotionally, she was living with the one-day-at-a-time precept.

"Hi, honey," Matt said as he threw open the door. "You're early, and I'm running late. The basketball game ran longer than usual."

Doria's eyes widened as they drifted over him. He was dressed in a maroon tank top that clung damply to his chest, and a pair of denim cutoffs that had to be a size too small. Her eyes traveled down his legs to his sneakers. They had so many holes in them that it was remarkable they stayed on his feet. Despite his ignoble sneakers, he was more gorgeous than her aerobics instructor, who was a contender for the Mr. Universe title!

"Who won?" she asked as she returned her gaze to his beloved face.

"The other guys, but only because I let them." He dropped a quick kiss to her lips. "Come upstairs. You can keep me company while I shower and shave. Sorry I'm running late, but I'll be ready in a flash."

"Matt, we don't have to go to the movies tonight," Doria said as she followed him.

"I promised to take you to the movies, and we're going to the movies," he declared.

"I just love it when you get macho," she drawled.

He entered his bedroom. "Wait until later, honey, and I'll show you just how macho I can be."

"Promises, promises," she teased.

"You'd better believe it," Matt responded as he stripped off his shirt and tossed it to the floor.

Doria picked it up with two fingers and carried it into the bathroom, tossing it into the hamper. "You're a slob, Matt. How hard would it have been to take your shirt off in here and throw it in the hamper?"

"If I'd done that, you wouldn't have followed me in here." He kicked off his shoes and shed his socks. Then he caught her waist and drew her toward him. "Want to take a shower?"

Doria pressed her hands to his muscled shoulders in token resistance. She'd never engaged in a more invigorating form of isometric exercise. "I've already had a shower, and we're supposed to go to the movies, remember? I wouldn't want sex to get in the way of your macho inclinations."

"We *don't* have sex. We make love," he corrected. He dropped another kiss to her lips, but this one wasn't quick. It was deep and slow and coaxing. When he tugged her toward him, she came willingly, awestruck by his hardness when their pelvises met.

He trailed his lips across her jaw to her ear, whispering, "My macho inclinations seem to be working just fine, but I think we should put them to the test, don't you?"

"What about the movie?" Doria asked breathlessly.

He slid his hand between them and went to work on the buttons on her blouse. "If we hurry, we can make the late show."

"If we do that, what will we do tomorrow night?"

"I'm sure my macho inclinations will think of something." He stripped off her blouse and then her bra, eyeing her breasts hotly. "Oh, they'll definitely think of something."

"Matt!" she cried hoarsely when he lowered his head and drew a taut nipple into his mouth, causing desire to shoot through her in a hot rush.

"Shower!" he gasped as he pulled away from her and stripped off the remainder of his clothes. Then he helped her quickly dispose of hers and hauled her into the shower. Beneath the warm spray, he taught her the many pleasures of aquatic lovemaking.

Much later, they lay entangled on his bed. When Doria sighed in satisfaction, Matt ran his hand down her back and asked, "What are you thinking?"

"That I like being with you like this," she answered.

"You mean you'd rather be lying in bed with me than sitting in the theater watching Patrick Swayze?"

"Well, now that you've reminded me of what I'm missing . . ."

Matt laughed and rolled her onto her back. He straddled her hips and tickled her sides until she was roaring with laughter. She tried to tickle him back, but he captured her hands.

He held them against his chest and smiled at her. "This is the way I like you best, Doria. All smiles and laughter."

"It's easy to laugh around you," she admitted.

He brought her hands to his lips, kissing her knuckles. "Laughter's been pretty rare in your life, hasn't it?"

"It's been pretty rare for you, too," she noted. "We've been too busy struggling to survive to find much to laugh about."

"Yeah, but we've made it, Doria. Now it's time for us to learn how to have fun. Real fun."

"And what's *real* fun?" she asked indulgently.

"Walks in the rain. Dancing in the street. Taking a ride in a hot-air balloon."

"Good heavens, Matt, you'll catch a cold, get run over by a car and probably crash to the ground!"

"Now, Doria," he chastised. "You have to be daring."

"I'll think on it."

"Good girl. Are you hungry?"

"That depends. Are you cooking?"

He arched a brow. "Is that a statement on my culinary skills?"

"Nope. It's a statement of laziness. I don't want to get up."

He climbed off the bed and slipped into his pants. "Then I'm cooking. Sandwiches okay?"

"Sounds fine."

When he was gone, Doria propped the pillows behind her back and studied Matt's bedroom. Like the rest of the house, it was in various stages of remodeling, though it was the closest to being finished. The heavy oak furniture was masculine but it was softened by the patchwork quilt that served as a bedspread. There were a few items of clothing strewn around the room, and there was the normal clutter of male paraphernalia on the bureau.

When Doria experienced a compelling urge to sort through that clutter, she brought herself up short. Matt might be her lover, but that didn't give her the right to paw through his personal possessions. Determined to steer her mind away from the temptation, she reached for the television remote control.

"Klutz," she muttered when it slipped from her hand to the carpet. She leaned over the side of the bed to retrieve it, but it was nowhere in sight. Grumbling to herself, she climbed out of bed and walked to Matt's closet, retrieving the robe she'd worn on several occasions. Then she knelt beside the bed and lifted the dust ruffle in search of the missing control. It still wasn't in sight, but she did find several books. Why would Matt keep his books under the bed when he had an almost-empty bookcase sitting in the corner?

She told herself that looking at the books was as much an invasion of his privacy as searching through his possessions. The temptation, however, was too great to ignore. She pulled one out, and her jaw dropped when she saw the cover. It was a romance novel! Certain that her find was a fluke, she dragged out several more books.

A guilty blush flared into her cheeks when Matt walked into the room, saying, "I hope you're hungry, honey. I've just created a masterpiece, and— What in hell do you think you're doing?" he barked when his gaze landed on her.

"Looking for the remote control," Doria answered. "When did you start reading romances?"

He scowled. "Who says I read them?"

"Come on, Matt. They're under your bed. If you're not reading them, who is? The mice?"

"I don't have mice." He slammed the tray of sandwiches down on the dresser, stomped over to her and dropped to his knees. Snatching the books off her lap, he stuffed them back under the bed. "All right, Doria. I read romance novels. What's the big deal?"

Doria drew her hand over her mouth to stop her twitching lips. "There's no big deal. It's just that you don't seem to be the, uh, type to read them."

"And what type reads them?" he asked belligerently.

She started to say the sensitive type, but stopped when she realized that Matt was sensitive. She then started to say a man secure with himself, but she'd never met a man more secure with himself than Matt.

She eyed him speculatively before saying, "A man like you reads them."

"Is that an insult?" he inquired suspiciously.

"No," Doria assured. She reached up and touched his cheek. "It's a compliment. You're a very special man, Matt."

"You're pretty special yourself," he stated gruffly. "I guess that's why I'm in love with you."

"Yeah. Well, help me find the remote control," Doria mumbled as she once again lifted the dust ruffle.

"Is that all you have to say?" he demanded as he snatched the material out of her hand. "I just told you that I love you!"

"What do you want from me?" she sniped. "An avowal of undying love?"

"You're damn right!"

"Well, you're not going to get it!"

"Why not? You love me, Doria. If you didn't, you couldn't make love with me the way you do."

"You know, Matt, that is the most arrogant, egotistical hogwash you've spouted to date. Just because I have sex with you doesn't mean I love you!"

*"We don't have sex!"* he yelled.

"Well, we sure aren't stealing hubcaps!" Doria taunted as she stood.

He scowled at her. "You're not ready to accept us yet, are you?"

"There's no *us,*" she wailed in frustration.

"Yes, there is," he said as he also stood. "We're in love, Doria."

"Matt, you've been reading too many romance novels. People don't fall in love in two weeks."

"We didn't fall in love in two weeks, Doria. We fell in love fourteen years ago, and that love never died. If it had, we each would have found someone else, settled down and started having families. Instead, we both held out. We knew in our hearts that we'd eventually find each other again. Now that we have, I think we should get married."

*"Married!"* Doria yelped. "Good Lord, Matt. You haven't just been reading too many romance novels, you've overdosed on them! We were kids, fourteen years ago. If we felt anything for each other, it was adolescent hormones. And the reason I haven't gotten married to someone else is because I don't want to get married to anyone."

"That's ridiculous, Doria. All women want to get married."

Doria gave a flabbergasted shake of her head. "I don't believe you said that. Not all women want to get married. In fact, a lot of us feel we're better off alone than putting up with a man, particularly if he's a Neanderthal like you!"

Matt crossed his arms over his chest and glared. "Are you saying that you'd rather spend your life alone than be married to me?"

"You'd better believe it," she retorted. "Even if I could dismiss your archaic attitude about women, we're too drastically different to make a marriage work."

"Give me ten examples of how we're so different," he challenged.

"All right. I go to the gym three times a week, you play basketball in the ghetto. I drive a car, you drive a motorcycle. I dress for success, you won't wear a pair of jeans without a hole in them. I eat in restaurants, you eat in diners. I hire bonded repairmen, you hire gang members. I keep a spotless apartment, you live in a demolition project. I curl up with a good mystery, you hunt down muggers and drug dealers. I go to dinner with friends, you risk your life prowling through bad neighborhoods with yours. I care about what people think, you prefer to shock them. I like landscape art, you like inkblots."

"Well, I'll be damned. You did come up with ten examples," Matt said in amazement.

"I'll be happy to go on it you'd like," Doria replied smugly.

"You don't need to go on, Doria. What you need to do is think about your answer. Except for your comment on art—and my paintings are abstract art, by the way, and not inkblots—every one of your reasons was related to image. You aren't living your life the way you want to live it. You're living it the way you think other people would live it. But it isn't their life. It's *yours*."

"Yes, Matt, it is mine, and you're trying to make me live your way," she declared defensively.

"No," he disagreed staunchly. "I don't want you to live my way. I just want you to live, and you're not doing that. You need to shake things up, honey."

"And how do you suggest I do this 'shaking up'?" she asked in irritation.

"I think the best way to do it is to go back to your roots," he answered.

"In other words, I should join this crusading group that you belong to and spend all my free time running around the ghetto tilting at windmills. Well, Matt, I'm not Don Quixote. I know when I'm facing a losing battle."

"You don't always lose, Doria, and when you win, it's an incredible feeling."

"That feeling is nothing more than ego," she pointed out dryly.

"Maybe it is, but it still feels good. Almost as good as loving you."

"Oh, Matt, why are you doing this to me?" Doria questioned with a troubled frown. "What do you want from me?"

"Everything," he replied simply. "I love you."

"But I don't want you to love me!" she exclaimed in distress.

"I know," he murmured as he drew her into his arms. "But eventually you'll trust me enough to accept my love, because nothing is going to make it go away, honey. Nothing."

Doria rested her forehead against Matt's chest and blinked against the sting of tears. She wanted to believe what he was saying, but her father had once loved her, too. If she couldn't trust in her own father's love, how could she ever trust in Matt's? She couldn't, and if she had one ounce of courage, she'd walk away from him before he could reject her.

But she couldn't any more walk away from him than she'd been able to walk away from her father. Where there was love, there was always hope, and she loved Matt irrevocably.

AS MATT EYED HIMSELF in the mirror, he decided that love should be classified as a severe mental disorder. If it wasn't, then why was he wearing a damn designer-label suit?

"Are you decent?" Raul asked as he knocked on Matt's bedroom door.

"That depends on what you call decent," Matt grumbled as he walked across the room and jerked open the door.

Raul let out a whistle. "Damn, you don't even look like yourself."

"Tell me about it. This idea of yours is nuts."

"Stop complaining, Matt. You said that Doria's biggest problem with your relationship is your life-styles. All you have to do is show her that you can fit into her world, and she won't have anything to complain about."

"What if she decides she prefers me in a suit?"

"Then haul her off to bed and prove to her that you look much better without one," Raul answered with a laugh. He handed Matt the keys to his Ferrari coupe. "The flowers are in the car, and your dinner reservations are for eight. Don't be late. And mind your manners."

"God, you're worse than my mother," Matt muttered as he headed for the stairs. "Take care of my bike, Raul. If there's one scratch on it, you're dead."

His mood brightened once he was behind the wheel of Raul's car. Its power was certainly greater than his bike's. When he pulled onto the highway and hit the accelerator, he was actually smiling.

And he had good reason to smile. Doria didn't know about the special night he had planned for them. He was going to arrive at her apartment and sweep her off her feet with the finesse of a romantic hero. He was going to prove to her that he could fit into her world and, hopefully, she in turn would realize that she would always fit into his. Their differences weren't really differences, but a matter of life-style. They could make those life-styles mesh if she would only lighten up and give him a chance.

As he neared her apartment, he braked at a stoplight and eyed the liquor store in the next block. A bottle of champagne would be a nice touch for his romantic evening, he decided. When the light changed, he swung into the parking space in front of the store and whistled a jaunty tune as he headed for the door.

"Well, hell!" he exclaimed in low anger when he walked inside and a young man with a gun swung toward him. He'd just stumbled in on a robbery—and Doria claimed *his* neighborhood was dangerous!

# 12

WHEN MATT WAS an hour late, Doria didn't think much about it. She figured he'd been playing basketball and had lost track of time. It certainly wouldn't be the first time it had happened, and she knew it wouldn't be the last.

There was a part of her that was deeply jealous of his devotion to his "kids." She recognized that the emotion was childish. How could she be jealous of a handful of kids who didn't even know where their next meal would come from?

When Matt was two hours late, she began to worry. She called his home but there was no answer. She got the answering machine at his office and hung up. She assured herself that he was on his way and forced herself to sit down and read the newspaper. A half hour later, however, she was pacing the floor. If Matt was going to be this late he would have called, so where was he?

Her mind conjured up a scene of his motorcycle flattened on the freeway. When it had gone through that exercise in minute detail, it conjured up an image of him bleeding to death in some filthy alley in the ghetto. That image stayed, because it was the most likely scenario.

*Damn!* Why did he insist on living on the fringes of hell? Why couldn't he accept that he'd made it out? Why did he have to keep going back?

Her frantic thoughts were interrupted by the buzz of her intercom. She ran to it and pushed the button. "Matt?"

"It's me, honey. Sorry I'm late."

"Not as sorry as you're going to be when I get my hands on you!" she muttered as she pushed the button to open the gate.

Then she threw open the door and watched him walk across the courtyard. He was limping, and she cried out in alarm when he walked beneath one of the spotlights and she saw his face. One eye was nearly swollen shut and he had a split lip. God, she'd been right! He might not be bleeding to death in an alley, but he'd definitely been mugged!

When he arrived at her door, he thrust a huge bouquet of wilted flowers at her, saying, "They're a bit worse for wear, but it's the thought that counts, right?"

Doria automatically took the flowers and crushed them to her chest as she gaped at him. He was wearing what looked like a suit. One shoulder had been ripped and the sleeve hung at his elbow. There were holes in both knees of his pants. The fabric was smeared with black streaks mixed with blood, and he smelled like a distillery!

"Matt?" she questioned hoarsely, unable to get out another word.

"I had a little trouble getting the champagne," he announced as he produced a magnum of champagne from behind his back and wagged it at her.

Doria didn't see the bottle, however. Her gaze was glued to his raw knuckles. Slowly she raised her eyes back to his bruised and battered face.

"Why, Matt?" she asked, her voice choked with tears. "Why do you keep going back? Can't you see that they're eventually going to kill you?"

"I wasn't in the ghetto tonight, Doria. I was in a liquor store three blocks away from here. I walked in on a robbery, and the kid wasn't very cooperative when I asked for his gun."

Doria shook her head, but she wasn't sure what she was denying—the fact that he'd been fighting crime in her own neighborhood, or that he'd once again rushed in where even fools feared to tread. She was also unaware that tears were rolling down her cheeks.

"Honey, don't cry," Matt ordered gruffly as he pulled her into his arms and hugged her tight. "I'm all right. Really, I am."

"I couldn't stand it if I lost you," she choked out on a sob.

Matt smiled against her hair. Considering the condition of his split lip, the small act hurt like hell, but it was worth the ache. It was the closest she'd ever come to making an avowal of love.

"You're not going to lose me," he assured as he backed her into her apartment and closed the door. He leaned against it and drew her between his thighs. "I'm invincible."

Instead of his words soothing Doria as he'd intended, they infuriated her. She jerked away from his embrace and glowered at him.

"You are *not* invincible, and it's time you grew up and faced that fact!"

Matt's own temper exploded and he pushed away from the door, his fists clenched at his sides. "Dammit, Doria, I'm sick and tired of you intimating that I'm childish!"

"I'm not *intimating* that you're childish. I'm stating a fact!" She continued before he could respond. "Last week you said you loved me and wanted to marry me, and you were mad when I refused. Well, this is one of the reasons why I did. If you get yourself killed playing one-man crusader, where does that leave me?"

"I wasn't playing crusader tonight," Matt objected. "I was an innocent bystander who happened to walk into the wrong liquor store at the wrong time."

"I'm sure that's true," Doria conceded. "But when you saw what was going on, did you stand meekly by with your hands in the air?"

"At first. But when I saw an opportunity to get the kid, I went for it."

"Tell me, Matt, if you hadn't 'went for it' would someone have been hurt, or was the kid on his way out the door?"

Matt didn't have to answer. The flood of crimson in his cheeks said it all. She gave a weary shake of her head. "I rest my case."

Matt regarded her silently for a long time. Finally he said, "I understand what you're saying, Doria, and I agree that I could have used better judgment tonight. The kid was leaving and I should have let him go. But when I'm in a dangerous situation, I don't stop to think. I react."

"And one of these days you're going to 'react' your way right into a grave!" Doria responded with vehemency. "Can't you close your eyes and walk away?"

Instead of answering, Matt said, "I had big plans for us tonight. I bought this suit." He glanced down at his torn clothes and grimaced. Then he glanced at the bouquet of flowers she'd dropped to the floor. "I bought you flowers. I borrowed Raul's Ferrari, and I made reservations at one of the most expensive restaurants in town. I planned to sweep you off your feet and prove to you that I could fit into your world if I wanted to."

He paused and sighed heavily. "Now I know that I was fooling myself. I can play the role, Doria, but it isn't me. I love you, but I can't change to suit you. I have to be what I am."

"I'm not asking you to change," Doria stated passionately. "I'm asking you to have more regard for your own safety. I'm asking you to take one moment to consider what you're doing before you react."

"I'll tell you what," Matt said as he scrutinized her. "I'll promise to think before I react, if you'll promise to stop fighting against our relationship and start looking for compromises to make it work."

"That's not fair, Matt. I'm talking about your life."

"So am I," he stated quietly. "Without you, I'm nothing."

"Oh, Matt," Doria whispered as new tears began to roll down her cheeks.

Matt walked to her and enfolded her in his arms. This time he didn't try to stop her tears, because he knew they were tears of love.

MATT CURSED as he came off the basketball court and glanced at his watch. He'd lost track of time and he was supposed to have been at Doria's fifteen minutes ago. He was going to be late. Again. She was going to be mad. Again. Damn, love was a pain in the neck! He quickly swiped at his face with a towel and then headed for the curb.

"Hey, Matt! Wait up," Raul called.

"I can't, Raul," Matt called back. "I'm running late and Doria's going to be spitting mad."

Raul chuckled as he jogged across the court. "I'm sure you can handle her."

"Ha!" Matt exclaimed scornfully. "Shakespeare had Doria in mind when he wrote *The Taming of the Shrew*. I'm telling you, Raul, don't ever fall in love. As soon as a woman knows how you feel about her, she turns into a nag."

"It can't be that bad, Matt. If it was, you'd dump her."

Matt grinned wryly. "Yeah, well, being in love does have some good points, too. What did you want to talk to me about?"

"I just wanted to make sure that you're still on as a chaperon for the professional wrestling matches."

"Damn. I'd forgotten all about them. It's the last week of this month, right?"

"Yeah. I know things are hot and heavy between you and Doria, and I hate to tie you up for the entire week. But I really do need you. There isn't going to be a problem, is there?"

*Oh, there will definitely be a problem,* Matt thought grimly. Doria was already complaining about the amount of time he spent with the kids. It irritated the hell out of him, but he recognized that she was afraid some harm was going to come to him. The only way he knew to reassure her was to get her involved in his work so she could see firsthand that what he was doing wasn't dangerous. Whenever he suggested it, however, she went through the roof.

Doria was still running from her past. He'd been telling himself that she just needed time, but he was beginning to worry that time wasn't going to be enough.

"There won't be a problem," he told Raul. He couldn't disappoint the kids just to soothe Doria's irrational fears.

WHEN DORIA FOUND herself fretting over Matt's late arrival, she forced herself to calm down. He'd called, so she knew he was safe. Besides, she needed to think about how she was going to approach him about her vacation.

They'd been dating for two months, and she'd have to be blind not to see how much he loved her. For the first time in her life, she could see the possibility of a future. The only obstacle in her path was the mythical past she'd created for herself.

She'd begun to understand that she had to tell Matt the truth. When she'd realized that her annual vacation "to visit her parents in Florida" was coming up, she planned to talk Matt into going out of town with her. They could go somewhere where it would be just the two of them. Then she'd find a way to tell him what she'd done and why she'd done it. If he loved her as much as she thought he did, he'd understand.

When the buzzer rang, she opened the security gate and then nervously rubbed her damp palms against the seat of her denims. She forced a smile to her lips and opened the door.

"How much trouble am I in?" Matt inquired.

"You're not in any trouble," Doria answered.

He eyed her warily as he walked inside. "You mean you're not going to screech at me?"

"I don't screech," Doria muttered indignantly as she closed the door.

"No, you don't." He tucked a finger beneath her chin and tilted her head up for a kiss. "You just get that haughty little tone in your voice that infuriates the hell out of me."

He dropped a kiss to her lips before she could respond, and any ire Doria felt was gone in a flash. He was here. He was safe. And he loved her. She wrapped her arms around his neck and kissed him with all the ardor inside her.

"Now, that's what I call a welcome-home kiss," he exclaimed as he drew away and smiled at her. "What's made you so amenable tonight?"

"I'm always amenable."

"I wouldn't touch that line on a dare." Tucking her against his side, he led her to the sofa. When they were seated, he said, "Okay, honey. Out with it. Something's up."

"You're right. I have a vacation coming up. I thought that we could go out of town together. Somewhere romantic where we can be alone."

"That sounds wonderful. When's your vacation?"

"The last week of this month."

Matt gave a resigned shake of his head. "I can't go out of town then, Doria. I've already made plans for that week."

"Can't you change them?" she asked plaintively. "Please, Matt. This is important to me."

"Honey, I can't," Matt replied as he caught her face in his hands and regarded her with regret. "I promised to act as a chaperon so we could take the kids to the professional wrestling matches that week."

Doria stared at him in disbelief. Then she batted his hands away as her temper flared. "You won't go on vacation with me because you want to take a bunch of ghetto kids to some dumb wrestling matches?"

"They're not dumb wrestling matches. They're professional matches. It'll be a treat for the kids."

"I don't believe this," Doria muttered as she jumped to her feet and began to pace. "I ask you to go on a romantic vacation, and you prefer to go to wrestling matches!"

"I didn't say I preferred it, Doria. I said I was obligated," Matt corrected. "I know you're disappointed, but we don't have to go out of town to have a romantic vacation. I'll take as much time off as I can and we'll do some special things together."

"I can't do that," Doria declared striding over to the window and staring out at the courtyard, so angry she wanted to scream and so hurt she wanted to cry.

"Come on, Doria, be reasonable," Matt coaxed as he went over to her and rested his hands on her shoulders. "I know you're disappointed, but we can have fun right here in L.A."

Doria gave an adamant shake of her head. "I *have* to go out of town."

"Why?" he demanded, finally losing his temper.

"Because I do!" she yelled, ducking beneath his arms and scooting away from him. She took several deep breaths before she said, "What's more important to you, Matt? Me or your do-gooder activities?"

"Dammit, Doria! You know the answer to that. *You'r* more important to me, but I'm not going to disappoint bunch of underprivileged kids when there's no reason wh you can't vacation in town."

"Fine," she said, tossing her arm into the air. "You go t your wrestling matches. I'll go on vacation alone!"

Matt swore vehemently. What she was pulling was out right emotional blackmail, and he wasn't going to fall fo it. "You know, Doria, there is another alternative. You coul change your vacation to a later date."

"I can't do that. We have audits scheduled for the entir year, and they're scheduled around our vacations. The onl way we can change it is if there's an emergency."

"Then we're at an impasse. I want to go out of town wit you, but I can't go that week."

"Someone could replace you as chaperon," she sug gested.

Matt shook his head. "I could probably find a replace ment for two or three nights, but not for the entire week."

"Well, at least I know my standing in your life," she de clared stiffly as she turned and headed for the kitchen. "Yo can leave, Matt. Don't let the door hit you in the rear."

Matt was so furious he was tempted to storm out. In stead, he closed his eyes and counted to a hundred. By th time he finished, he'd reduced his temper to a low boil. He' also come to the conclusion that there was more going o here than was apparent on the surface. Doria could b maddening, but she wasn't superficial. For her to begrudg a bunch of kids a good time, there had to be a reason.

"I thought I told you to leave," she snapped when Mat walked into the kitchen.

She was sitting at the table, and Matt pulled out a chai across from her. "You did, but I'm not leaving until you tel me exactly what is going on here. Why are you so insistent about going out of town?"

"Because I can't let anyone see me here!" she railed without thinking. When she realized what she'd said, she let out a groan, propped her elbows on the table and buried her face in her hands. Before he could question her, she said, "Everyone at the office thinks I'll be in Florida. I can't take the chance of someone seeing me here."

"I see," Matt responded, though he didn't see at all. "Why are you supposed to be in Florida?"

Doria leaned back in her chair and raked her hands through her hair. "This is supposed to be my yearly sojourn to Florida to visit my retired parents."

Matt stared at her in bewilderment. "What in the world are you talking about? You don't have retired parents in Florida!"

"All my friends and coworkers think I do," Doria stated with a harsh laugh. "They think Doria Sinclair grew up in a nice, middle-class family with all the middle-class trappings. She's an only child, and her retired parents live in Florida."

"You created nonexistent parents?" When Doria nodded, he asked, "What kind of ridiculous game are you playing?"

"I'm not playing a game," she answered staunchly. "It's a matter of self-defense. Respectability gains respectability, and growing up on the streets isn't respectable."

Matt was so dumbfounded that it took him a minute to find his voice. "Doria, your perspective on respectability is askew. Where you come from doesn't make you respectable. It's how you live your life."

"You're wrong, Matt," Doria disagreed fiercely. "My first day in college I watched the cliques begin to form. There was *them* and there was *us*. If you were from the ghetto, you

were one of *them*. Everyone looked at you with pity or di
trust. If they did make friends with you, it was because the
parents had told them not to associate with people like yc
and they were going to show their parents they could c
whatever they wanted. I decided that I would never be or
of *them*. I was always going to be one of *us*."

"So you made up nonexistent parents."

"I made up an entire life."

"You've been living this lie since college?" When Dor
nodded again, he questioned, "No one knows the truth?'

"Just you, my father and his doctor. Well, the FBI know
They had to do a security clearance on me."

"I can't believe this," Matt declared as he gave a daze
shake of his head. "How long did you think you could g
away with it?"

"I can get away with it forever," Doria replied. "Peop
only know what you tell them, Matt."

"But it's a lie, Doria. *Your whole life is a lie!*"

"No," she disagreed. "The first eighteen years of my li
are a lie. Everything I've done since I walked out of th
ghetto is the truth."

"Except your vacations to Florida."

"All right. One week out of every year is a lie."

Matt gave another dazed shake of his head as he stare
at her. As the import of everything she'd said began to sin
in, he suddenly understood why she refused to work in th
ghetto. She'd have to align herself with a group of men an
women who had all come from the streets. By joining, she'
be one of *them*, and she was ashamed of her roots. Then h
realized that if he carried that one step further, it meant sh
was also ashamed of him.

Matt didn't want to believe that was the case, but h
found himself asking, "Doria, if you and I were at a part

with people from your office, would you be embarrassed if I told them I grew up in the ghetto?"

Doria didn't answer, but her pained expression and guilty blush said it all.

Matt knew he should be angry, but oddly enough, he felt sorry for her. He also recognized that until she could accept who and what she was, she would never be happy, and no amount of love he could give her would change that.

"You know, Doria, I knew you had problems," he told her. "I just never understood how serious they were. You've convinced yourself that you have to live a lie to be respectable, but true respectability comes from integrity and honesty."

When she opened her mouth to reply, he held up his hand and continued. "You proved that you have integrity when you went to your boss and told him about us, even though you knew it might cost you your job. But you have a long way to go when it comes to honesty, because you're not only lying to your friends and coworkers, you're lying to yourself."

When she again tried to speak, he again held up his hand. "If you really want people to believe that you have retired parents living in Florida, then you should fly to Florida and find some to adopt, because lies always have a way of catching up with you."

"Matt—" she began, but Matt shook his head as he climbed to his feet.

"I love you, Doria, but I can't be with a woman who's ashamed of me."

Doria was stunned as she watched Matt walk out without a backward glance. It wasn't until the front door closed that the reality of what had happened began to set in. She'd told him about her lie, and instead of forgiving her, he'd walked out on her!

She wanted to burst into tears, but she forced herself t be angry instead. It was easy for Matt to sit in judgment o her. He'd escaped the ghetto and been able to build a bridg of respectability between his old life and his present one. anyone asked him where he came from, he could always sa Denver. He could even give a respectable address in a re spectable neighborhood to prove his claim. All she'd eve have to offer was a rat-infested hovel!

She tried to hold on to her anger, but as she wandere through her apartment, everywhere she looked there was memory of Matt. Maybe she should move. In fact, mayb she should transfer to another state. There, she could buil a new life for herself and become an entirely new person.

That was exactly what she'd do, she decided as sh headed for her bedroom. While she was on vacation, she' fly to Florida and check out the IRS offices there. She coul always say that now that her parents were older she wante to be closer to them. It was the perfect alibi, especially nov that Matt was no longer going to be a part of her life.

The reality of that hit her as she stared at her unmade bed The pillow Matt had slept on last night still bore the im print of his head. Matt was gone again, and this time h wouldn't be back.

She picked up the pillow and hugged it to her chest. The she lowered her head and wept.

MATT WELCOMED the fast-paced, no-holds-barred basket ball game. It was exactly the rough-and-tumble type of ex ercise he needed to work off the tension that had bee building inside him since he'd walked away from Doria tw days before.

Several times he'd been tempted to call her, but he' managed to stop himself. There was no way he could han dle her being ashamed of him, and he feared that if she aske him to come back, he might succumb. In the end that would destroy him, because he couldn't pretend that he wasn't exactly what he was—a street kid who'd made it with a lot of blood, sweat and tears.

By the time the game was over, Matt was bruised and exhausted, but he felt better. He grabbed a towel and mopped the sweat off his face. When he looked up, he would have sworn that Doria was leaning against the basketball pole next to the street. He blinked, certain he was imagining her, but when she started walking toward him, he knew she was real.

Matt regarded her warily, telling himself that even if she begged him to come back, he had to refuse. He *had* to!

When Doria reached Matt, she forgot the carefully rehearsed speech she'd been practicing for the past twenty-four hours. As her gaze roamed over his face, she realized that regardless of whether they'd been friend or foe over the past few months, there had always been one constant between them: love.

As a teenager, her love for him had been different, and in some ways it had been stronger, because he'd been the first person she'd ever felt safe enough with to love. But then he'd left. Only now, when it was possible that she'd lost him forever, did she understand that when Matt had been sent away, she had started running and hadn't been able to stop.

Her thoughts were interrupted when Matt curtly asked, "What are you doing here, Doria?"

"I thought it was time to come home. Would you like to take a stroll down memory lane with me?"

Before Matt could respond, she turned and walked toward the street. He stared after her in indecision, but curiosity finally spurred him into following.

He caught up with her and they walked several blocks silence before Doria said, "You know, this isn't the neig borhood we grew up in, but it looks the same, doesn't it?

"Yes," Matt answered. "That was one of the first thing noticed when I started coming here."

They continued on for several more blocks before Dor said, "I've been doing a lot of thinking the past couple days, and I suddenly realized that there's no shame in bei poor. It is shameful, though, that there's such poverty in land of plenty."

"I agree completely," Matt replied. "But we can't treat th disease, Doria. We have to treat the symptom, and that's lack of education. The more of these kids we can get in school and keep there, the better chance we have of wipir out the ghetto environment."

"Do you think that the group of professionals you b long to would have room for another crusader?" Doria c sually asked.

Matt's heart skipped a beat at her question. He told hin self not to read too much into it as he cast a sidelong glan at her. Her expression was impassive.

"They probably do," he replied noncommittally. "But you're thinking of joining, Doria, you'd better consult wit your parents in Florida. They might take exception to th fact that their daughter is claiming to have grown up in th ghetto."

Doria came to a stop and gazed up at him. "My paren in Florida have been put to rest, Matt."

"And how did the people at your office react to their de mise?"

Doria gave a nonchalant shrug. "I'll probably be th scandal of the office for years to come. Yesterday I went t work and told everyone the truth about my past. And mean the entire truth, Matt. Right down to the details of my juvenile record."

Hope flared in Matt's chest; but again he told himself not to read too much into her words. "And how do you feel about telling them the truth?"

"Oh, I'm sure I can handle that scandal. It's the second one I'm not so sure about."

When she didn't deliver the punch line, Matt prompted, "Okay. I'll bite. What's the second scandal?"

Doria knew that the rest of her life depended on her next few words. She almost chickened out, but she refused to let herself start running again.

"I told everyone at the office that I'm engaged to Matthew P. Cutter, CPA, who dresses like James Dean, and in his younger years was one heck of a car thief."

Matt's lips twitched as he reminded, "*You* stole the cars, Doria."

Doria laughed as she tossed her arms around his neck. "I'm just protecting your ego, Matt. After all, if people find out you used a girl to steal your cars for you, you'll be the laughingstock of all our friends and coworkers."

"I suppose you're right." He wrapped his arms around her waist and pulled her close. "I've missed you, honey."

"I've missed you, too," Doria said tearfully as she rested her cheek against his chest. "I know I've been positively wretched, but I love you, and I promise you that I'm going to change."

"I don't want you to change, Doria," Matt told her as he caught her chin and raised her face to his. "I just want you to come to grips with your past so you can be happy."

Doria nodded. "I know, and one of the ways I'm going to do that is to see a counselor. My first appointment is next week."

"It'll be tough at first, honey. But I'll be there to help you through it."

"I was hoping you'd say that, and since you have, when do you think we can get married?"

Matt chuckled as he tucked an errant curl behind her ear. "As soon as we can get a license. I'm tired of my soon-to-be wife being the scandal of the office."

"I love you, Matt."

"Oh, honey, I love you, too," he murmured huskily as he dropped a sweet kiss of promise on her lips.

As they walked back to their cars, Matt asked, "How did you find me?"

"I stopped by your office and talked to Uless."

"Damn, that's what I need to do!" he exclaimed.

"Matt, what are you doing?" Doria demanded in confusion when he dragged her to a sudden stop.

"Wait right here," he told her as he dashed across the street and into a corner grocery. He returned a few minutes later with a pack of cigarettes and a book of matches.

"Oh, Matt. You haven't started smoking again!"

"Nope." He opened the pack and pulled out a cigarette. He lit it, took one puff and then dropped it to the street, crushing it with his sneaker.

"What was that all about?" Doria questioned in bewilderment.

"The only way I can give Uless his five hundred bucks is to let him win the bet. You're my witness. I was smoking."

"Why didn't you just give him the money?" Doria asked with a chuckle.

"That's charity, Doria. The leader of the Sinners would never accept charity."

"You know, Matt, for a hood, you're a pretty nice guy."

"Yeah, well, that's a secret you're going to keep, right?"

"Don't worry. I'll defend your blackguard reputation."

"Good. That means I can tell you about the sunflower seeds."

"Sunflower seeds?"

"Oh, honey, it's a long story. Let's go home so I can tell you all about it."

*Home!* The word shimmered through Doria and she finally understood its concept. Home was where the heart was, and her heart belonged to her wonderful, respectable hoodlum.

## *A Note from* Carin Rafferty

When I first sat down to plot *The Hood,* all I knew about my hero was that he'd grown up on the streets. It took me several agonizing hours to come up with his name, but once I did, Matt was instantly alive. Matt is one of those rare heroes that pops into a writer's life and writes his own story. Whenever a scene wasn't working, it was invariably because Matt had dug in his heels and said, "I will not do that!" I quickly learned to give Matt his lead, and not once did he disappoint me. What I think I love best about Matt is that there is no pretense. He knows where he's been, where he's at and where he's going. He's tough around the edges, but there's a wealth of caring and commitment to him that makes him a knight in shining armor. And how could you not fall in love with a hoodlum who's addicted to sunflower seeds and romance novels? Matt will always hold a special place in my heart, and I hope that after reading his story, he'll hold a special place in yours, too.

**Books by Carin Rafferty**

HARLEQUIN TEMPTATION

281—I DO, AGAIN
319—MY FAIR BABY
363—SHERLOCK AND WATSON
373—CHRISTMAS KNIGHT

HARLEQUIN AMERICAN ROMANCE

320—FULL CIRCLE
359—A CHANGE OF SEASONS

RRL-1

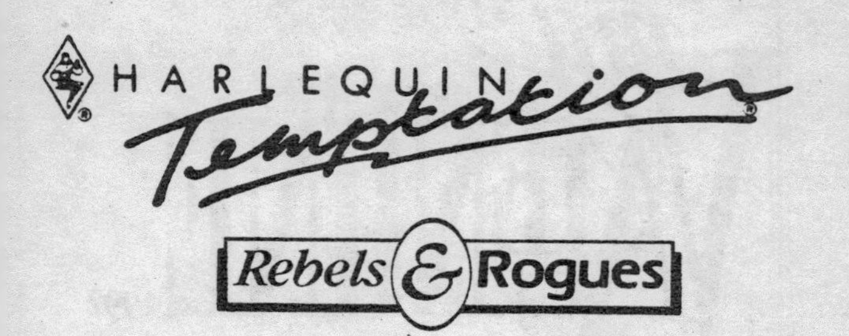
HARLEQUIN
Temptation
Rebels & Rogues